DEADLY MISTAKE

Cody pushed aside the curtain and leaned out to peer toward the bunkhouse and barn. He hadn't heard a horse, which meant that the killer was on foot. He wouldn't get away this night. Tonight the man in black's reign of terror would end.

Suddenly two arms shot up from beneath the window. Viselike hands clamped on to his shoulders, the fingers digging in like claws. The hands yanked the Ranger from his feet, pulling him out the window. His right wrist slammed against the windowsill as he was hauled through and sent hurtling to the ground. His fingers went numb, and the Colt fell from his hand.

The Ranger hit the ground facedown, and the impact drove the air from his lungs and dizziness into his head. . . .

Cody's Law

Ask your bookseller for the books you have missed

CODY'S LAW
Book 10

A GALLOWS WAITING

Matthew S. Hart

 Producers of **The Holts, The Patriots,**
and **The Frontier Trilogy: Westward!**

Book Creations Inc., Canaan, NY • Lyle Kenyon Engel, Founder

BANTAM BOOKS
NEW YORK • TORONTO • LONDON • SYDNEY • AUCKLAND

A GALLOWS WAITING

A Bantam Domain Book / published by arrangement with
Book Creations Inc.

Bantam edition / January 1994
Produced by Book Creations Inc.
Lyle Kenyon Engel, Founder

ISBN: 0-553-29767-8

Published simultaneously in the United States and Canada

PRINTED IN THE UNITED STATES OF AMERICA
RAD   0 9 8 7 6 5 4 3 2 1

A GALLOWS
WAITING

CHAPTER
1
||||||||||||||||||||||||||||| ||||||||||||||||||||||||||||

The killer stood in the deep shadows that clung to the loblolly pines. The glow of lanterns that ringed the meeting grounds was too feeble to penetrate the cloaking darkness; even the silvery light cast by a full October moon failed to cut through the pines' dense needles.

Here, swallowed by the night, the cool air bathing his face, the killer felt safe and secure as he watched those who'd gathered for the preaching slowly say their good-byes and leave. He felt an old urge stirring—a hunger that he'd suppressed since the end of the Civil War. For many years the urge had lain dormant. Now it had resurfaced.

His right hand slipped into his coat pocket and caressed the curved blade of a skinning knife. This, too, reassured him, and he smiled. He looked toward the circle of lanterns surrounding the meeting that was breaking up, and his gaze homed in on a young woman who was saying her farewells to the others. She started off toward town, clutching a small reticule in both hands as she moved beyond the lanterns' quavering glow.

The killer readied himself.

Suddenly the woman vanished in the deep shadow cast by a copse of trees. The killer caught his breath; his temples began pounding. Where was she? Was she now lost to him?

As suddenly as she had disappeared the young woman reappeared, stepping from the black shadow into the dim moonlight. The killer breathed with relief and smiled again as he watched her continue on toward town. Her pace was steady; her head was slightly hung as though she was studying the ground, either for footing or lost in thought.

And those thoughts? The killer could well imagine what was going on in the woman's mind. He had watched her while the preacher delivered a sermon extolling the bounty once found in a basket of seven fishes. The young woman's eyes had been rapt with devotion. Her look had ignited the hunger that the killer had long renounced.

But he renounced it no longer.

His fingertips slid over the coolness of the curved blade. Laughter drew the killer's attention back to those still milling about the meeting grounds. No one moved for buggy or horse, but he sensed his opportunity grow short. Soon the lingerers would begin to head for their homes. That would increase the chance of discovery, and that couldn't be risked. If the hunger was to be satisfied, now was the time to move.

He stepped out of the pines.

Like the woman, the killer walked with his head slightly bent toward the ground. But his eyes weren't downcast; they were focused on the woman's back, yet aware of the town's lights that grew brighter with each step.

This place was so perfect. Texarkana, its residents called this fledgling community built on each side of the Red River. Or rather, two communities—one above the river in Arkansas and the other below the river in Texas—that shared a common name. Arkansas and Texas. It was in Arkansas, when he was fifteen, that the killer had first taken human life, when his hand had closed around the skinning knife's rough horn hilt for the first time. And it was in Texas after the war that he had hidden from his craving. This community, claiming both Texas and Arkansas, spoke to all that had gone before and all that was yet to come. . . .

Darting into the shadows of a sycamore, he watched the young woman open the gate of a picket fence surrounding an unlit whitewashed house, then enter the neatly kept yard. Four strides along the flagstone walk brought her to the front porch, two more steps delivered her to the front door. She entered her house, closing the door behind her.

The killer stepped from beneath the tree, anticipation making the air alive as though a thunderstorm were brewing. Reaching the fence, he stopped again as the yellow glow of a single lamp finally lit a curtained window. The killer smiled. He had chosen well. The young woman had introduced herself to the visiting circuit preacher as a spinster schoolteacher, which meant that unless she had, say, a relative living with her who was already asleep in the darkened house, she lived alone. He wouldn't have to search for someone else that night.

Boldly he stepped from the shadows, opened the fence gate and crossed to the house, and knocked. His pulse quickened with familiar expectation as footfalls sounded, coming toward the door. There was a rustle just on the other side of the door, the handle turned, and the door inched open.

"Oh! It's you!" The young woman's puzzled expression immediately transformed into a smile. "Your knock took me aback. This is a pleasant surprise. I wasn't expecting visitors." A nervous laugh broke her words for a moment, but then she added, "To be honest, being a spinster, I seldom receive visitors."

"I'm sorry to bother you," he replied. "But I wonder if I might trouble you for a glass of water." He smiled. "It's been a long night that will stretch three times as long if I have to walk all the way into town with a parched throat."

"It's no trouble at all." She opened the door wide. "Won't you come in?"

"I won't be disturbing anyone?" he asked cautiously as he stepped into the hallway. The faint fragrance of rose water mingled with cedar filled the house. The smell reminded him of a young girl's hope chest.

"There's no one to disturb. I'm quite alone," she replied with a friendly smile. "Just follow me to the kitchen," she invited. "I have an indoor pump."

He pulled the door closed behind him. One hand slipped into his coat pocket and freed the curved-bladed knife, and as the young woman stepped across the kitchen's threshold, his other hand shot out and clamped firmly over her mouth, silencing her scream as he drew the skinning knife across her throat.

With the pumping gush of crimson he took the first step back on the path of madness.

CHAPTER

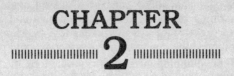

|||||||||||||||||||||||||| 2 ||||||||||||||||||||||||||

Sam Cody pulled out his pocket watch. For a moment the tall Texas Ranger weighed the big turnip-style watch in his palm, finding satisfaction in the watch's heft. Maybe it was a matter of simple familiarity. For a man who spent half his life in the saddle, often working undercover assignments with assumed identities, there were few constants.

He opened the watch and studied the sepia-toned photograph of a beautiful young woman in her early twenties— roughly ten years younger than himself—framed within, wondering as he had a thousand times just who she was. Strangers usually assumed she was his sweetheart or sister. In fact, the photograph had been in the timepiece when he'd acquired it for the purpose of hiding his badge— which fit neatly behind the photograph in the left-hand side of the case—while working undercover. Today, though, he wore that five-pointed encircled star, hand carved from a Mexican ten-peso piece, pinned openly to his leather vest.

"Straight up noon," Cody announced, then returned the watch to its pocket. He tapped his silver spurs to the side of the big lineback dun to quicken the horse's pace.

"Damn!" Harlan Brown muttered. He cuffed back his wide-brimmed hat and wiped his sweaty blond hair, then squinted at the sun that dominated a cloudless sky. "It ain't even close to the heat of the day, and I feel like I've been bakin' in an oven for hours. In all my twenty-one years I can't remember a hotter autumn. What month is it supposed to be, anyway?"

Cody gave the young rancher a doleful smile. If the sweat staining his work shirt a darker blue and dripping down his rugged face was any indication, the mercury had already topped the ninety-degree mark and would probably continue to climb for hours.

"October," the Ranger replied, wiping his hand across his thick, dark mustache. "Didn't you notice Jack Frost painting the leaves on those trees back yonder a mile or two?"

The rancher scowled. "The only jack I've seen's been jackrabbits. And I ain't noticed nothin' a man could rightly call a tree—not even an overgrown bush—since me and Carolina moved down from Austin last year."

"I reckon trees *are* a mite sparse in this country." Cody's gaze swept over the low-rolling hills around him.

Here near Eagle Pass all of Texas seemed to gradually slope toward the Rio Grande and the Mexican border. The alkaline soil was better suited for producing rocks than grass, and the main vegetation was gnarled, thorny chaparral brush. There were far more hospitable portions of Texas to live in, and when men like Harlan Brown settled this land, dug in, and scratched out a living, it never ceased to amaze Cody. That these men not only managed to provide for their families but often prospered spoke highly of their grit.

"Everythin's sparse in this country." Harlan tugged his hat low again. " 'Cept rustlers."

"Hell, son, men throwing a wide loop aren't restricted to this land. Anyplace one man's got a cow, calf, or steer, another man's likely to come along and try to take it from him if there's a profit to be made. Sometimes even when there isn't. There are those who just have to take."

"These thievin' whoresons took more than a cow or a steer." Harlan spat to the ground from the back of a bay. "They made off with half my herd!"

Rustlers were what had taken Cody fifty miles south of Del Rio, headquarters for Company C of the Texas Rangers Frontier Battalion. For two weeks he had patrolled the area, hoping to find fresh tracks that'd lead to the rustlers who had been hitting the region for the past six months. Twice he had done just that. The tracks had played out on the sandy bank of the Rio Grande—on a direct line to Mexico across the river. Like the tracks, he'd stopped at the water's edge. The star pinned to his vest meant nothing south of the border.

The rustlers were likely from across the river near Piedras Negras, Cody figured. If he had to put money on it, his bet would be that they were small ranchers trying to increase their own stock by "borrowing" from their northern neighbors. In fact, both Texans and Mexicans living in the borderlands commonly raided each other's herds when extra beeves were needed.

Until the rustlers struck Harlan's place, they'd limited their raids to a dozen head at a time, spreading their strikes across the region and never hitting the same rancher twice—facts supporting Cody's belief that the men he tracked were small Mexican ranchers rather than hardened outlaws set on making a quick profit. The raids had followed a set pattern: Hit an isolated herd near the border, drive off a few head, then ride straight for the Rio Grande.

The rustlers had broken that pattern when they'd struck the Brown ranch. For one thing, they'd ridden deep into Texas. For another, they'd gotten greedy, taking fifty head of cattle. It was those two mistakes that Cody hoped to turn into advantages—for himself. Men couldn't move a large herd as quickly as they could a dozen head, and sixty miles into Texas meant that the rustlers faced days rather than hours to their border escape. The raid had taken place three nights before. Cody had hooked up with the rancher early the next afternoon, and the pair had been on the rustlers' trail ever since.

"Creek up ahead." Brown stood in his stirrups and pointed. "They must've had rain in these parts in the last day or so. Creeks've been dry at home since August."

"Your stock's getting thirsty," Cody answered. "This is the first water we've come across in a day and a half. If they weren't watered, they'd start dying."

From the corner of an eye the Ranger saw the young rancher's face go stone hard at the prospect. Rustlers driving cattle until they dropped dead in their tracks wasn't a pretty picture—especially if those cattle belonged to you.

Calling the water a creek turned out to be an exaggeration. It was more like a lazily trickling ribbon in the middle of a wide sandy bed. But it *was* water. Reaching it, Cody halted and dismounted, and while the dun drank the muddy flow, the Ranger knelt and cupped a palm into the trickle to drink, too. Though the water was half grit, it was wet and washed the dust from his mouth and throat.

Pulling a bandanna from a back pocket of his jeans, Cody dipped it into the water and washed the sweat and dirt from his face. He then bathed the back of his neck as he stood and surveyed the desolate terrain. The stream continued its serpentine course southward, wandering through the low hills. The tracks followed the stream. The rustlers apparently intended to keep to the creek, using the surrounding hills to hide their movement. If they stayed with the—

The Ranger suddenly frowned. He looked at the ground, his gaze darting from side to side. Kneeling, he brushed his fingertips over the hoofprints at his feet.

"Harlan, you notice anything strange about these tracks?" he asked, his frown deepening.

The rancher glanced up from where he knelt to drink and glanced around. He shook his head. "Nope. They look like the trail we've been followin' for two days. Nothin' different about 'em."

"Yep." Cody nodded as he edged back his Stetson. "That's exactly the way they struck me."

Harlan shoved to his feet as the Ranger's meaning sank in. His head jerked from one side to the other. "This don't look right. If those sons o' bitches had watered my stock here, the tracks would be more spread out and confused lookin'. Hoofprints pointin' ever' which way."

Cody nodded thoughtfully. "Just what I figured. But these tracks keep right on going, just like they've done since leaving your spread. The rustlers didn't stop here. They pushed your cattle on." He pointed downstream. "They kept on in that direction."

"Damn!" Anger filled Harlan's voice. "Don't those bastards know they'll kill my stock if they don't water 'em?"

"They must know. But they don't seem to care." Cody examined the tracks once more. Then his pulse quickened.

His tired eyes noticed the first good news they'd seen in two days. "Some of these tracks still have water pooled in 'em."

"So?" Harlan asked impatiently.

"You said yourself. The heat's like an oven. How long would you reckon water in a shallow hoofprint would last, baking under this sun?"

The young rancher glanced at the sun, then looked back at the tracks. "No more'n an hour at most."

"That's the way I read 'em," Cody said. "Your herd's an hour, maybe less, ahead of us. A half-hour hard ride should get us to it."

Harlan nodded toward the horses still drinking from the stream. "Got any idea where we can get fresh mounts? These two won't last another half hour without rest."

Cody eyed the lathered animals. His companion was right. They hadn't ridden the horses hard, but they'd pushed them for nearly two straight days with no more than short breaks, even at night. While a horse was stronger and faster than a man, a man's endurance was greater. Cody's dun and Harlan's bay appeared near the limit of equine endurance.

"We'll walk 'em a while. Say, a half hour to give 'em a breather. We can't risk longer than that," he added. "The border's no more than two or three hours away. If they reach the river with your cattle, there's nothing we can do about it."

Under usual circumstances Cody wouldn't have hesitated to cross the Rio Grande and retrieve the stolen cattle. It was a sure way to put a quick end to the months of petty rustling. But the circumstances were anything but usual.

Mexico was once again claiming that Texas, once its northernmost province, rightly belonged to it, having been stolen by criminals back in 1836. Rumors abounded of the Mexican government gathering an invasion army to retake Texas, and though no armed troops had appeared to challenge Texas's sovereignty, tensions had grown taut and strained along the border. That the politicians in Washington paid no heed to the threat did little to ease Texans' fears. To those born in the Lone Star State, Mexico's boasts were very real. Its troops had sporadically invaded Texas soil, once pushing all the way to San Antonio and taking that city before Ranger companies and a ragtag army of farmers and ranchers drove them back across the Rio Grande.

Which meant that for now there'd be no riding below the border to apprehend rustlers. Before he'd left for Austin to meet with Frontier Battalion commander Major John B. Jones, Company B's Captain Wallace Vickery had given strict orders that no man in the company was to cross the Rio Grande—no matter what the circumstances.

"If the government in Mexico City got wind there was Rangers ridin' around down in Coahuila, it just might be the spark needed to set 'em off. No man of mine is goin' to set off that spark," Vickery had said. "And if fear of bein' the man who starts a war ain't great enough to keep you out of Mexico, then think this over: I promise to personally skin any man I hear of slippin' across the river."

The tone of Vickery's voice had made it clear he wasn't making an idle threat. In spite of his mounting years, the old Ranger was as tough as a barrel of nails. He was also a man of his word.

Cody looked at Harlan, who said, "We walk for a half hour, then we ride—hard. I want my cattle back."

Slipping the reins over the dun's head, Cody nodded and turned downstream. "Let's walk."

Within ten minutes he regretted that decision. The sun was hot enough for a man on horseback; on foot it had his shirt drenched in sweat before he covered a quarter mile. And his boots hardly eased the situation. Their thick, arched heels were made to fit a stirrup; they weren't made for hiking.

"Cody, do you really think we've got a chance of gettin' my cattle back?" Harlan asked as he walked beside the Ranger.

"To be honest, I wouldn't have placed hard-earned greenbacks on our chances an hour ago," Cody replied. "But we're close. A lot closer than I thought." When the rancher's worried expression didn't change, he added, "We've got another thing working in our favor. Odds are those rustlers are already counting unhatched chickens. They've gone two days without trouble. They're probably imagining

themselves free and clear on the other side of the river. If
we play our cards right, we'll take 'em by surprise. Catch
a man with his pants down, and he won't put up much of
a fight."

The young rancher smiled uncertainly. He nodded, but
the gesture lacked conviction.

"Something eating at you, Harlan?"

Harlan glanced up at the tall Ranger, then quickly looked
away. His right hand rose to lightly brush the butt of a
Remington revolver that jutted from the holster on his hip.
"I've had plenty of practice with this and the Winchester
back there on the saddle. But that's what it's all been,
practice. I never had the need to throw down on a man."

Cody understood Harlan's uncertainty. The question of
whether the rancher would be able to fire when he stared
into the eyes of another man would be answered only when
the situation arose. Still, he tried to waylay the young man's
worries.

"I'm not going to lie to you. Having to stand facing a man
twists your gut into knots and leaves you wanting to empty
your stomach of every meal you've ever eaten in your life."
A sideways glance revealed that Harlan found little solace
in those words—not surprisingly. Cody tried again. "It gets
down to these brass tacks: When a man comes gunning for
you, how much in the right you are or how wrong he is
makes no nevermind. Only one thing matters—kill or be
killed. There's no other choice."

The rancher pursed his lips and nodded. Cody knew how
hard the decision Harlan faced was; it didn't grow easier
with the passing of time.

"Like I said before, there might not be a need for gun-
play. If we keep our cards close, I think we can take 'em
by surprise," Cody concluded.

He had no sooner uttered the words when they rounded
an abrupt turn the creek made, entered a wide, grassy draw
fed by several other small streams, and saw Harlan's cattle
loosely spread out, grazing on the lush vegetation.

Cattle weren't the only thing in the draw. Six riders
ringed the small herd, and a startled yell from a mounted
man on Cody's right announced the presence of the two

unexpected intruders. The riders immediately wheeled their mounts around and spurred toward Harlan and Cody.

"Reckon we've found what we're looking for," Cody said. Stepping to the dun, he yanked a Winchester '73 from its saddle boot and cocked the lever-action repeating rifle.

"Tell me what you want me to do," Harlan said, a nervous quaver in his voice.

Cody answered curtly, "Shoot straight."

The young rancher's right hand dropped to his holstered Remington.

But Cody gestured toward Harlan's bay. "Try your rifle first. It'll give you better range."

The rancher's cheeks flushed as he shoved the revolver back into leather and stepped to the bay's side. Following Cody's lead, Harlan freed his own Winchester and cocked it.

Slapping the dun on its rump to send the animal out of harm's way, Cody turned to the charging riders and shouldered the Winchester.

The sharp crack of a pistol rent the air, and the angry whine of lead whistled over the Ranger's head as the closest of the rustlers opened fire. The remaining five riders followed suit, pulling their handguns and firing them at arm's length.

Harlan shooed his horse away and spun around, fumbling to retain a hold on his rifle as the hail of bullets bit harmlessly into the ground. The rancher's eyes were wide, and he swallowed hard. His hands shook as he lifted the Winchester to his right shoulder.

"Take a steadying breath and stand your ground," Cody instructed. "A man on horseback is more likely to hit you by accident than on purpose. He's being jostled around too much to get off a clean shot." The Ranger sighted down the barrel of his rifle, his right forefinger curled around the trigger. "Take the right and work inward. I'll take the left."

As the horsemen fired another round, the Ranger drew a bead on a bearded rider to the far left. The man's worn and faded clothing confirmed Cody's speculation that the cattle thieves were just Mexican ranchers rather than *pistoleros* seeking misbegotten fortune north of the Rio Bravo. It would've been simpler if the six had kept their revolvers holstered and made a run for the border and freedom, but it was too late for simple solutions now; the six had made their decision. That choice left Cody with but one course to follow. He squeezed the trigger.

The bearded rider jerked upright as the Winchester's slug slammed into the center of his chest. He went down, tumbling head over heels and finally sprawling facedown in the ankle-deep grass.

From the corner of an eye Cody saw a second gunman slump to the neck of a black-and-white paint as Harlan's first shot found its target. The sombreroed rustler's body slid from the saddle and dropped to the ground. No longer driven by its rider's spurs, the paint veered wide to the right.

Cody swung his Winchester and sighted in on a hatless rustler, who thumbed back the hammer of his pistol and pointed it at the Ranger standing directly in his path. Cody squeezed off his second shot at the exact instant the rustler fired.

Heat like a glancing brush with a hot skillet seared across Cody's left shoulder. The rustler's bullet had found a target. The same couldn't be said for the Ranger's shot. The horseman continued to urge his sorrel gelding forward.

Cody gritted his teeth against the pain he knew would momentarily lance into the shoulder and snapped a fresh cartridge into the Winchester's chamber. Sighting down the barrel, he brought the hatless rider into his sights. For the third time in less than half a minute the rifle barked.

This time the Ranger's aim was true. The hatless rider sagged in the saddle. His pistol fell from his hand as he grasped a broad, Mexican-style saddle horn for support. It did him no good. His horse swung to the left, and the sudden lurch was enough to unseat the gunman. He spilled to the ground, dead or dying.

"Damn!" Harlan cried out as he got off his second shot.

A fourth rider tumbled from the saddle as Cody turned to find the young rancher holding his right thigh with both hands.

"I've been hit!" Pain and fear filled Harlan's eyes as they found the Ranger's. "I'm bleeding!"

The young man's wound would have to wait. If Cody didn't take out the two remaining gunmen, either Harlan or he—or both—would likely be dead.

Levering another round into the chamber, the Ranger focused on the pair of riders—and found that he couldn't get off one accurate shot, let alone two. The horsemen, no more than twenty yards away, were driving straight for the lawman and the rancher, ready to let their mounts' hooves accomplish what their bullets had failed to do.

Not even wasting the time to squeeze off a certainly useless shot, Cody dropped the Winchester and launched himself at Harlan, who still held his bleeding leg. Cody tackled the young man around the waist and hit the ground, rolling just beyond the lethal hooves.

He released his hold on Harlan and continued to roll until he was well out of harm's way. His right hand dropped to his hip and pulled the .45-caliber Frontier Colt from its holster. Cocking the hammer, the Ranger sat up and took aim at his target, a middle-aged man dressed in peon white and wearing a ragged straw hat and sandals.

Cody's first shot caught the rustler in the side of the head as he reined his chestnut around for another charge. Without so much as a grunt of surprise, the gunman slumped to the neck of his mount and lay there as the horse trotted toward the middle of the draw.

The last of the cattle thieves died as he reined a dappled gray around and swung his pistol wide, searching for the Ranger. He never got a bead on his target. Cody's Colt spat lead a second time. The slug slammed dead center into the rider's chest. An expression of shock and disbelief crossed the man's face an instant before he fell from the saddle.

Still holding his gun at the ready, Cody pushed to his feet and cautiously approached the last of the six rustlers to die. The man, who appeared just a few years older than Harlan Brown, lay on his back. His chest was still, and he didn't move when the Ranger nudged him with the toe of a boot. Certain the young rustler was dead, Cody turned to check on the other five.

"You're bleeding!" Harlan called, lifting a bloody hand and pointing at the Ranger.

Instantly Cody wished the rancher hadn't opened his mouth. Now his left shoulder began to throb and burn. He cocked his head to the side and strained to see the wound. Blood had turned the torn edge of his blue work shirt purple. Beneath the rent he saw an angry-looking line of bloody flesh. The bullet had grazed the shoulder, gouging out a quarter-inch gully as it passed.

Cody's gaze shifted from his wound to Harlan. "I'll live. What about you?"

The rancher gave a sheepish shrug. "I guess I'm okay. I've never been shot before. I think my leg hurts a lot worse than it looks. Slug entered here"—he pointed to a spot on his thigh—"and came out about an inch away."

"Got some sulfur powder and bandages in my saddle-bags," Cody said. "Soon as I check these other five, I'll take a look at that leg. It should be all right if we can keep it from festering."

"I'll be damned, Cody," Harlan said a short time later as he settled himself in his saddle. "I can barely feel it. The leg's a mite sore, but that's about it."

Cody grinned as he turned to mount the lineback dun. He didn't doubt the young rancher was feeling no pain. After washing Harlan's wound with the medicinal whiskey he kept in his saddlebags, he'd handed the bottle to the young rancher. Harlan had downed half the pint in two hearty swallows.

"Glad to hear it," Cody replied. "It'll stiffen up a bit, but I think it'll be all right." He winced in spite of himself as he swung into the saddle. His own shoulder had begun to stiffen. "Just keep the wound clean and use a heap of that sulfur I gave you each time you change the bandage."

"And change the bandage at least once a day," Harlan said, repeating the instructions the Ranger had previously given him.

Cody nodded, hoping his companion would be able to remember what to do after the whiskey wore off. Even a small injury could end up killing a man if he let it fester. "Time we were heading out. We got what we came for. No sense wasting time."

Harlan surveyed the grassy draw. He methodically looked at each of the six dead rustlers; then he looked at the Ranger. "You gonna just leave 'em here?"

Cody nodded again as he tugged the brim of his Stetson low. "This is where they decided to die. We'll leave 'em where they fell."

"That's mighty cold, ain't it?" Harlan gazed up at four buzzards circling high above. "Shouldn't we bury 'em and say some words or somethin'?"

"If you think they'd do that for us if it were you and me laying out there, then I'm willing to wait while you dig six graves and quote Bible verses over them," Cody answered. He then turned to the cattle grazing across the draw. "On the other hand, there's at least five hours till sunset. We can cover a lot of ground in that time."

Harlan's expression said that the idea of leaving the six didn't sit well with him. But he finally heaved a sigh and said, "I reckon you're right. They'd've left us for buzzard bait if the tables'd been turned."

Fact was, Cody would've liked to tie the rustlers' bodies across the backs of their horses and driven the animals across the Rio Grande into Piedras Negras as a warning to other would-be thieves. But tensions between Texas and Mexico being what they were, six dead men flaunted in Mexican faces might be the spark needed to ignite all-out war—and Cody had no intention of striking steel to flint.

"I think I can manage the herd by myself," Harlan said as he reined his bay around. "You probably got business elsewhere to tend to."

Though Cody was more than ready to ride back to Del Rio, he didn't feel right about accepting the young rancher's offer. "I'll ride with you for a bit. If that leg doesn't start acting up on you and the cattle keep their manners, then I'll think about heading back."

Harlan grinned. "Thanks, Cody. Thanks for everythin'."

CHAPTER
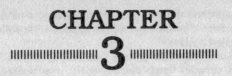
3

The saloon's batwings swung wide as two men with less than steady gaits strolled out into the San Antonio night. The larger of the two men maneuvered awkwardly down the three wooden steps leading to the dusty street. His companion leaned against a hitching post for support and laughed.

"Joshua, you watch where you're steppin' tonight. I wouldn't want my new business partner slippin' down and breakin' his damn-fool neck!"

The man called Joshua echoed his friend's laughter. "Hell, Sam, I'm not that drunk. We just had ourselves a bucket of beer—"

"Each," the one named Sam interjected.

Joshua brushed aside the comment with a wide, wobbly swing of his arm. "Don't mean nothin'," he said, his words a bit slurred. "I tell ya, I'm not that drunk, Sam. Never been so drunk that I couldn't manage to walk m'self home. Hell, a man that gets that drunk might as well be shot. Ain't no good to nobody, even himself."

Sam laughed again. "If you say so, Joshua. If you say so."

"Don't you worry none. See ya bright and early, Sam." Joshua waved a good-bye, drew himself as straight as possible, and started toward the San Antonio River, with its ancient cottonwood trees lining both banks.

From the shadows across the street from the saloon the

killer watched the two men part company, a pleased smile on his face. Stepping out of the shadows, he followed the one called Joshua.

Joshua. The killer's smile froze as his fingers found the curved skinning knife nestled in his coat pocket. *Joshua.* The name burned in his brain. That was his stepfather's name. It had all started with his stepfather.

Resolution guiding his steps, he strode off after Joshua.

He shivered again at the name. It had all started with his stepfather and his damnable hickory rod. Joshua.

He could still hear his stepfather's voice thundering with the fury of a raging storm as he'd pointed to a chair in the center of the woodshed and ordered, "Bend over and grab that chair! Do what I say, or I'll flay every inch of skin from your body. I promise you that!"

How many times had that demon in man's form taken him to the woodshed and beaten him? Over how many years? The memories blurred in the killer's mind. He could feel again the length of wood biting into his tender flesh, raising bloody welts in a crosshatch pattern on his back and legs. But he had held out—held out against the pain until his body and soul could no longer endure.

In the end, though, the killer had done as ordered. His young body battered and bruised, his spirit broken, he had given in to his stepfather's demands. Given in to Joshua.

The name brought him back to his present purpose. Ahead of him, the drunken man with the same name as his old tormentor was just a few yards ahead of him, lurching into the stand of cottonwoods on the bank of the San Antonio River. There he stopped and stood unsteadily, as if deciding what to do next or trying to remember why it was he had gone there. Gripping the skinning knife, the killer smiled and quickened his pace, then stepped directly in the man's path.

"Huh?" Joshua gave a start and shook his head. "Where the hell'd you come fr—"

His words died in a strangled gasp as the killer struck. His knife rose and fell viciously, over and over. Then, the hunger within him finally sated, the killer leaned down and methodically began to carve.

•   •   •

A trail-weary Captain Wallace Vickery carefully brushed
the dust from his flat-crowned black hat and then his black
broadcloth coat as he reached the outskirts of Del Rio. The
aging Texas Ranger straightened his string tie, then himself,
sitting almost impossibly erect in the saddle as he guided his
brown gelding into the border town. Vickery glanced at the
Ranger badge on the lapel of his coat, then gave it a quick
swipe with a sleeve. It didn't gleam like it did after a good
polishing, but still, the star glinted when it caught the sun.

Vickery didn't look as pressed and creased as he did
in his Sunday pulpit suit, but he was presentable. The
commander of Company C of the Texas Rangers Frontier
Battalion believed strongly that the men in his command
should be presentable in appearance and manner. Though
he had nothing against a man sporting facial hair—he himself was proud of the thick, white mustache covering his
upper lip—he insisted that it be kept neatly trimmed. Going
unshaven was not the same as wearing a beard, in the
captain's mind.

A Ranger's pay wasn't enough to outfit him, but Vickery
expected his men's clothing to be clean within reason. Dirt
and patches might be all right for some poor sodbuster
trying to scratch out a living in this inhospitable country,
but it wouldn't do for a Texas Ranger. Rangers had a long,
proud history in Texas, stretching back to when the state
was an independent republic. Vickery wanted those who
wore a Ranger badge under his command to do nothing to
tarnish either the badge or the history behind it.

"Mornin', Cap'n," called a shopkeeper from an open
doorway as Vickery rode slowly along the dusty main street
toward the large adobe building that housed Company C.
"Hot enough for ya?"

"And then some, Howard," the captain answered. He then
tipped his hat to two elderly ladies exiting a seamstress shop
on his left.

A couple of barefoot boys wielding rough whittled wood-
en pistols paused in their mock battle when they stepped
from a narrow alley that ran between two buildings. One

of the boys called out, "How was your trip to San Antonio, Cap'n Vickery? Run into any Comanches?"

Vickery shook his head. "No Indians this time 'round, boys. You two hold down the fort while I was gone?"

The other child pointed back into the alley. "Musta kilt us a hundred or two warriors back in the pass there. Think they escaped the reservation up at Fort Sill in the Indian Territory."

Vickery smiled and threw the youngsters a crisp salute. "Job well done, men! Keep up the good work!"

The boys returned the salute, then darted back into the alley with toy pistols raised.

Vickery's sharp blue eyes followed the children for several seconds, his amused smile slowly fading. There was a time when he *had* ridden forth to battle with Comanche, Kiowa, and Apache, but those times now often seemed as archaic as the massive Texas Paterson Colt holstered on his hip. It was the same pistol, now modified to accept cartridges, he had worn in 1838, when he first joined the Rangers. In those days he'd been as young as the new Lone Star nation of Texas. He'd held no rank, just been a simple Ranger patrolling the frontier near San Antonio.

He sighed. The captain's badge on his chest often seemed to weigh more than the Colt and cartridge belt around his waist put together. Ninety-nine times out of a hundred when assignments came up, he found himself handing them to men decades younger than himself. His own time, more often than not, was relegated to managing an ever-increasing river of paperwork that flowed across his old, scarred desk.

As he continued down the street he continued to smile confidently at passersby, but Vickery couldn't avoid feeling that he was some old warhorse who'd been put out to pasture. Company C was right in the thick of things, yet he felt passed over. The last two weeks had done nothing to lessen that feeling.

He wasn't certain what he'd expected when Frontier Battalion commander Major John B. Jones had summoned him to San Antonio. He surely hadn't been prepared to discover that all of Major Jones's Ranger captains had been gathered in the Alamo city. The meeting was the kind Vickery hated. It had nothing to do with renegade Indians or desperadoes terrorizing the land. Jones had assembled the captains in an attempt to draw up a rock-solid proposal for the continued funding of the Texas Rangers that the major could place before the state legislature. What Vickery had hoped would be a call to action turned out to be nothing more than politics.

Politics! Vickery spat the word in his mind. Politics wasn't why he'd accepted his command. Certainly the Rangers had his full support, and someone needed to fight for higher pay and better conditions for men courageous enough to choose the life of a lawman. He just didn't figure it had to be him.

As surely as he had been called to be a man of the cloth delivering the word of the Good Book, Vickery firmly believed that God had also endowed him with a strong will and an equally strong back to help make this land known as Texas a place fit for decent men and women to live.

If God had only given me some of Job's patience, Vickery thought ruefully. The four days and nights he'd spent on the trail from San Antonio hadn't done a thing to improve his patience, either, especially now that he'd reached the end of that trail. He had nothing to look forward to except all the paperwork he was certain had piled up during his absence. He sighed again. Like it or not, by accepting the command of Company C, he'd traded a horse and saddle for a desk and chair.

Reining in the gelding outside the low-slung adobe headquarters building, the captain dismounted and called for someone within to come and care for his horse. At least he enjoyed *that* privilege of rank, he thought to himself.

But there was no response to his summons.

The lines that furrowed Vickery's brow deepened as he frowned. "Alan? Seth? Howard? Cody?"

The frown darkened to a scowl as he looped the gelding's reins around a hitching rail. No sound came from inside headquarters. That wasn't natural. The men in Company C were high-spirited individuals. Usually when his men weren't joshing each other, they were sharing details of assignments. Something was wrong for things to be so quiet.

Edging back the tail of his coat, Vickery eased the five-shot Texas Colt from its holster. He thumbed back the hammer and leveled the pistol while he inched toward the building's closed door. As he reached for the latch with his left hand, he pressed his back to the wall, making sure he was out of the direct line of fire. Shoving the door inward, he jerked his arm back to elude the gunfire he was certain would greet him.

Nothing happened.

Surprised, Vickery pulled off his hat and tossed it through the open doorway. Still no gunfire. Either the building was empty or whoever was inside was playing his hand close. *Only one way to find out,* the Ranger captain decided, and he rushed through the door, Colt leveled and ready.

Vickery's gaze shot from side to side. He lowered the Colt and carefully eased the hammer down. No band of hardcases held the company hostage. No outlaw was holed up inside. In fact, no one was inside. Vickery frowned again. An empty headquarters left him more puzzled than he'd been a second before.

Holstering his revolver, Vickery strode through the building to his office. Nothing there provided an answer to his unvoiced question, either. Everything seemed to be in order—in fact, more orderly than usual. The reports, papers, and wanted posters that normally cluttered his desk were missing; only a single sheet of yellow paper was lying there.

Crossing to his desk, Vickery picked up the paper, which was a message signed by his second-in-command, Lieutenant Oliver Whitcomb. The frown returned to his weathered face as he began to read. By the time he finished, Vickery wished—for the second time in less than an hour—that he were a cussing man.

He dropped the sheet of paper to the desk and settled into his chair. *Missed out again,* he thought. According to the note, three hours earlier Whitcomb had led every available man in the company northward along the Rio Grande to intercept a troop of Mexican soldiers that had reportedly crossed the border.

"And left me here to stare at these old walls," Vickery said aloud.

The Ranger captain stared forlornly at his desk. Minutes earlier he had fretted about facing a mountain of paperwork. Now it appeared that Whitcomb had managed to handle all the reports without him. Vickery shook his head. In all probability Whitcomb's mission was another in a dozen false alerts that Company C had answered in the past six months. Still, the slim possibility of seeing action was far better than sitting behind a desk, twiddling one's thumbs.

Leaning back in the chair, Captain Wallace Vickery closed his eyes and sighed. He'd have been more likely to see action while helping Major Jones draw up a budget proposal than he was here. Letting his weariness overcome him, he nodded off to sleep.

"Captain? Captain Vickery?"

Vickery's eyes flew open, and he found himself staring up into the face of José Todd, Del Rio's telegrapher.

"Takin' a li'l catnap, Captain?" José grinned at the Ranger, who edged his chair away from the wall and let all four legs settle to the floor.

"More'n a nap." Vickery rubbed a thick hand over his face to wipe away the sleep. "Passed out like a babe. Was havin' myself the strangest dream."

"Dream?" José cocked an eyebrow. "Your dreams sometimes have hidden meanin's."

Vickery smiled and shook his head. "Not this one, my friend. This one was more like an old pleasant memory. There was this young gal I met when I first joined with the Rangers. She used to make doughnuts whenever I came a-callin'. Fancy kind, sprinkled all over with cinnamon and that powdery sweet sugar."

"Confectioner's sugar," José offered.

"Reckon so. Never knew what it was called. Guess that's where I got my taste for doughnuts, though."

Vickery smiled at the memory of those almost-forgotten

days. He hadn't thought about Florabelle Carter in ten months of Sundays. At one time he'd hoped to give her his name; then that young rancher from down near Corpus Christi came along and popped the question first. Florabelle up and got married before he knew what'd happened.

"I never heard nothin' about doughnuts in dreams meanin' somethin', Captain." José scratched at his chin and looked perplexed.

"Doubt if it means anythin' 'cept to me." Vickery smiled wistfully. "Now, what can I do for you, José?"

The telegrapher shook his head. "Ain't what you can do for me, it's what I brung for you. Major Jones sent you a wire from San Antonio. Don't reckon I ever received a message this long before—it's more like a letter. Must'a cost him a golden eagle to send."

Vickery's head snapped up at the mention of Jones's name. "Why didn't you tell me you had a telegram from Major Jones instead of standin' there talkin' like some fool about doughnuts and dreams? Let me see that goldurned telegram, José!"

"It wasn't me that started talkin' about his dreams and how much he likes doughnuts," José grumbled, pulling out the telegram from a back pocket. "From the way it reads, it sounds like you Rangers have run up against a demon with this one, Captain. Yes, sir, a real hell-spawned demon."

Vickery snatched it from his hands. "I don't need a review of my own telegram, José. I can read it myself." Vickery held the first page of the two-page wire at arm's length. After he finished the second paragraph, he looked up at the telegrapher. "José, seein' as how you were the one that received this here wire, I know you probably got most of it memorized by heart."

"Not by heart, but I know the gist of it," José admitted with a nod.

"Well, if you know what's good for you, you better forget that gist. Understand?" Vickery's eyes narrowed as he stared at the telegrapher.

"You mean I can't even tell my Maria?"

" 'Specially not your wife! A man might as well take out a front-page advertisement in the county newspaper as tell Maria!" Vickery pointed a finger at the telegrapher. "I want your word, José, that what's in this telegram won't go beyond this room. This here's official Ranger business. If word of this got out, it could interfere with our work and maybe get one of my men killed."

José swallowed hard. "Reckon I never thought of it that way. You got my word on it. I clean forgot what was in that wire."

"Thank you, José. Now, I need to be alone to study this."

"Yes, sir." José tipped his hat. "But you remember what I said: That's a hell spawn described there, not a man."

José left the office, and Vickery began to slowly read the two-page message. As he got further into the telegram, the Ranger decided that the telegrapher hadn't been harsh enough in his assessment: "Demon" hardly described the man capable of the murderous acts detailed in Major Jones's report. Four butcheries of human beings were outlined, each more grisly than its predecessor. Vickery's stomach lurched as he read of the slain schoolteacher in Texarkana. By the time he finished reading the description of a rancher killed in San Antonio the night before, his gut was churning with horror and disgust.

Jones's lengthy telegram ended by noting that each of the brutal murders corresponded to the route of a Johnson Line stagecoach traveling from Fort Smith, Arkansas, to El Paso, Texas. The possible connection between the stage and the murders hadn't been discovered until an hour after the coach had left San Antonio that very morning. The last line of the message read:

WITHOUT DELAY ASSIGN MAN UNDERCOVER TO INTERCEPT STAGE, AS CERTAIN IF KILLER IS PASSENGER, AND APPREHEND.

Hell spawn. José's words echoed in Vickery's mind while he carefully reread the whole communiqué. Coming again to the last line, he read Jones's command aloud. " 'Without delay assign man undercover to intercept stage, ascertain if killer is passenger, and apprehend.' "

The major's orders had Sam Cody written all over them, Vickery told himself as he put down the telegram. How many times in the past had Vickery sent that lone wolf Cody undercover? And how many of those times had Vickery wished that it were he and not Cody riding out of Del Rio on assignment? More times than Vickery had wanted to admit to himself. Until now.

The Ranger captain smiled. Though he'd never say it to Cody's face, the younger Ranger had always reminded Vickery of himself in earlier days—a mite stubborn and single-minded at times, but with the grit to back it up when the need arose.

"'Without delay,'" the captain read aloud once more. His smile grew to a grin. The assignment might have Cody written all over it, but Cody wasn't here. In fact, the only Ranger in sight was himself—which meant that he'd have to tackle the assignment himself.

The twinge of guilty pleasure Vickery felt for deciding to personally handle the mission dissipated when he read the last line of Major Jones's telegram yet again. The choice wasn't his; he was simply following the orders of a superior officer. Written orders at that, he thought.

Vickery looked up at the map of Texas hanging on the wall facing his desk and traced an invisible line almost due north from Del Rio to the town of Sonora. Eighty miles as the crow flies, he estimated. If he rode hard through the night, he could easily reach Sonora before the stagecoach pulled in there on its westward journey.

A plan formed in Vickery's mind. In Sonora he'd buy himself a ticket and become a passenger on the stagecoach. As far as an undercover story went, he wouldn't have to break any of the Ten Commandments to come up with one: He'd claim he was a circuit preacher on his way to El Paso. The Ranger-cum-preacher nodded with approval. His cover story might not be the out-and-out truth, but it wasn't a lie either . . . leastwise, not a total lie.

Feeling an excitement he hadn't experienced in a long time, Vickery pulled out a pen, ink, and paper and began to write a quick report. He'd leave the message and Major Jones's wire on the desk for Lieutenant Whitcomb.

CHAPTER
4

Cody lifted the lineback dun's right-rear hoof. It didn't take a blacksmith to determine why the horse had come up lame. The shoe was loose. The Texas Ranger brushed away a pea-sized stone lodged between shoe and hoof.

"Damn!" Cody said, releasing the dun's ankle and straightening. He turned and stared into the animal's eyes. "I can almost believe you somehow planned this just to see me walk the last three miles into town."

The dun snorted.

The limping horse had reason to be ornery. The stone had bruised the hoof like it'd bruise a man's heel. The horse had probably picked up gravel from the loose shoe, which then got wedged way into the hoof. There was no way a man could cut the stone out; nature had to take its course. Time would eventually work the stone upward until it popped free of the hoof at the coronet band.

Regardless, Cody had to complete the return to Del Rio on foot, and the dun would be out of commission for a few weeks. The Ranger hoped there was a spare mount in the Company C stable. Though the state of Texas didn't equip Rangers with their own horses, tack, pistols, or rifles, much less clothing, lodging, and food, it did at least provide each company with a few extra mounts, recognizing there were a million things that could go wrong with a horse. Trouble was, those few extra mounts were rarely enough to cover the men with injured horses, so if a Ranger came up on the short end, he had to either rent a horse from a livery stable or buy a second mount. Either proposition was expensive for lawmen who received wages only slightly higher than those of ranch hands—and ranch hands usually had room and board provided.

Looking optimistically at his situation, Cody hoped that after two straight weeks of patrolling the border he'd have no need of a horse for a while. He was, after all, overdue a few days of rest and relaxation. And besides, ninety-nine percent of Texans were good, God-fearing people who never caused a lick of trouble.

It was the other one percent that kept Cody and every other lawman in the state busy.

Cody stared across the stretch of terrain that led to Del Rio. Its largest building—the Rio Grande Hotel—was discernible even at this distance. As soon as Cody reported in at headquarters, the Rio Grande was exactly where he intended to be.

The hotel was the closest thing he had to a home. It was an equitable arrangement: He kept an eye on the place for the hotelier, discouraging barroom fights—or breaking them up if need be—and in exchange he got free lodging. Cody pictured a big tub of steamy water; the thought of sinking down in a hot tub and scrubbing away the accumulated trail dirt was about the finest thing in the world he could imagine. About.

Cody grinned as the image of Marie Jermaine formed in his mind. There was no way he'd rank soap and a hot bath above the fiery French redhead. The bath, however, would make it a damned sight easier to get close to the Rio Grande's hostess.

And should Marie be otherwise occupied with another man, as was sometimes the case—a paying client was as important as a special friend, after all—there was always Hope Baxter. The blond physician, recently arrived in Del Rio to assist her ailing uncle in his practice, was more than a little intriguing to Cody—a feeling that was mutual.

With the image of two tantalizing women vying for him, the tall Ranger made his way into the dusty border town. Logistics as much as anything brought Hope's beautiful face into focus in Cody's mind when he entered Del Rio.

Since her office was on his way to headquarters, it'd be a waste of boot leather to pass by, then return later just to say hello. And a delay in reporting in wouldn't be of any consequence. The rustlers he'd been assigned to stop weren't going to be bothering Texas ranchers ever again.

Reaching the Baxters' clinic, Cody tied the lame dun to a hitching post and strode toward the house. His foot was on the first step of three that led to the porch when he spotted a note tacked in the middle of the door.

Gone to the Jensen Ranch to deliver a baby. Mother Nature sets our hours today. Drs. Baxter.

So much for a neighborly hello, Cody thought as he turned and walked back to the waiting dun. He untied the horse and continued down the street toward headquarters, ignoring the regret he felt. After all, there was no need to be disappointed; Marie still waited at the Rio Grande Hotel. He hoped that his report to Captain Vickery wouldn't take too much time. Marie Jermaine was by far a more desirable companion than the Texas Ranger commander.

But the only sign of life Cody found at Company C was one brown gelding in the stable and a few flies buzzing in empty rooms. Perplexed, the Ranger made his way to Vickery's office. There on the desk he found the message from Lieutenant Whitcomb, the communiqué from Major Jones, and the note from Captain Vickery, all of which answered the question of where everyone was. His face darkened as he read Major Jones's communiqué. Even for a man accustomed to facing hardcases who placed no value on human life, the crimes described in the telegram left Cody sickened. This was no ordinary desperado; this was a bloodthirsty madman.

Going after the butcher who had murdered four people between Texarkana and San Antonio was the type of assignment Cody usually drew, but he didn't doubt Vickery's ability to handle the situation. A seasoned veteran, Vickery always seemed to have a few tricks up his sleeves to amaze cocky younger Rangers.

Lieutenant Whitcomb's note, however, made Cody apprehensive. A strict disciplinarian who would've been more at home with U.S. Army rules and regulations than the far looser Ranger organization, Whitcomb was capable of leading the men of Company C, should they encounter a hostile Mexican force. But his resolute belief in military tactics sometimes got in the way of a solution, to Cody's way of thinking—which had led to more than one fierce clash in the past between the two men.

Replacing the reports on the desk, Cody had a decision to make. Should he ride out and join the rest of the company on patrol for Mexican invaders, or should he remain in Del Rio and man headquarters in case an emergency arose? As much as he wanted a few days' rest, the tug of duty said he should attempt to join the company.

On the other hand, the odds were that Whitcomb and the men were on a wild-goose chase. With the fear of a war with Mexico running rampant along the border, it seemed that each week brought a sighting of "soldiers" pushing across the Rio Grande. Cody had ridden to meet these invasions on six occasions, only to discover the supposed soldiers were Mexican farmers hauling corn and beans northward for sale.

The Ranger wiped a weary hand over his face. He needn't choose a course at that very moment. The gelding in the stable was Captain Vickery's mount. Since, according to the captain's message, he had barely gotten back himself before heading out again, that meant the horse needed a night's rest as much as Cody did.

He reached a decision: He'd try to join Whitcomb and the others in the morning. One night in town was better than nothing, Cody thought as he stood up. And as soon as he tended to the dun's bruised hoof, he could begin enjoying that night.

The young desk clerk looked at Cody blankly when he asked for his room key. "Your name, sir?"

"Cody," the Ranger answered. He'd never seen the man before.

"Cody?" The clerk looked puzzled for an instant; then he abruptly smiled. "Oh, yes! Now I remember. Mr. Palmatier mentioned you had a room here. You're with the Rangers, aren't you?"

"Yep. Ernest or Emily around?" Cody asked, inquiring about the hotelier and his wife.

"Were for the better part of the morning. But when word of the wagons coming in got around, they asked me to fill in at the desk till they got back. My name's Jed Haltom, by the way. My father just bought the feed and seed. We moved out this way from Gilmer about two weeks back."

That explained why he'd never seen the young man before, Cody realized. What with Hope Baxter, all of Company C, and the Palmatiers absent, and a stranger at the hotel desk, he had started to think there was no one in town he knew. "What wagons?" he asked, suddenly reminded that he didn't know what the clerk was talking about.

Jed jerked a thumb over a shoulder. "About five rolled in from Mexico City this morning. Filled with dry goods, especially fabric and lace, they tell. Mostly female stuff like dresses and shoes. They're parked up at the other end of town. About every woman in Del Rio went to see what's new in styles—and nigh on every husband went with them to keep them from spending too much."

"Wise move," Cody said with a grin. "Is Miss Jermaine in?"

Jed shook his head. "She went off with Mr. and Mrs. Palmatier. Should I tell her you're in when they return?"

If Cody had expected even a friendly "howdy" to welcome him back to Del Rio, he was plumb out of luck. "I'd appreciate it. Meanwhile, I'd like a tub and enough hot water to float a four-masted schooner brought to my room."

"I'll have it brought up as soon as the water's ready," Jed promised.

"I could also use a steak about this thick"—Cody held thumb and forefinger about an inch apart—"and I want it *cooked*. I don't want it trying to get off the plate and run away from me."

"One well-done steak," Jed said. "Anything else?"

"A mountain of fried potatoes, frijole beans, and a pot of coffee. That should just about do it."

"I'll have a tray brought up with the bath," Jed replied earnestly.

Cody nodded and walked upstairs to his room.

When the tub and hot water arrived—followed almost immediately by his dinner—he sharpened his razor on a strop nailed to the wall. While two young boys filled the tub from wooden buckets they'd brought from downstairs, Cody filled a basin with the steaming water and set about scraping off three days' growth of whiskers. By the time the last of the buckets had been emptied into the tub, the Ranger had shaved and worked his way through a dinner that left him feeling full and satisfied. As soon as the two boys left, closing the door behind them, Cody stripped off his clothing, tossed it into a corner, grabbed a bar of yellow soap, and slipped into the big galvanized tub.

He sighed with pleasure as he settled into the bath. A man could keep himself and his clothing clean enough on the trail if he found a stream swollen with fresh rains. But standing naked as a jaybird in a cold creek with knees knocking and teeth chattering was a far cry from the luxury of a hot bath.

Cody ducked his head beneath the water for a moment, then applied the bar of soap to his hair. He worked up a thick lather before moving downward to scrub every inch of his body. When he had cleansed away all hint of the trail, he sank beneath the water once again to rinse away the suds.

"*Mon cher,* you remind me of a playful seal I once saw in a New Orleans zoo," a teasing voice said when the Ranger's head came out of the water.

Cody chuckled as he wiped the water from his eyes. "Marie! The boy at the desk said you'd gone shopping."

"I had," confirmed the beautiful redhead in a green dress standing in the doorway. She stepped inside, then closed and locked the door behind her. "I spent far more money on silk and lace than I should have. They are items best enjoyed in the bedroom."

"Sounds mighty interesting. Any chance I could talk you into trying 'em on for me?" In spite of their long history as lovers, Cody was always amazed anew by Marie's beauty whenever he returned to Del Rio after a long absence. The prospect of her modeling her purchases doubled the beat of his pulse.

Marie smiled flirtatiously. "I thought we might amuse ourselves with that later. At the moment I was considering taking a bath myself. It has been a long, hot day."

Cody grinned. "It so happens I think I know just the place to fill that need."

"Is that an invitation?"

"A matter of Texas hospitality."

Marie's acceptance came in the form of her fingers slowly undoing the hooks of her dress. Her eyes burned with an unmistakable pride while she watched Cody's gaze devouring her. When at last she stood naked before him, she posed briefly, turning to one side and then the other, obviously enjoying the pleasure the Ranger found in her body.

"Is the water hot?" she finally asked, her voice husky.

Cody held out a hand for her. "We'll make it hotter."

She came to him.

Captain Vickery sat on a wooden bench outside the Johnson Stagecoach Line's Sonora office, shifting his weight from one side to the other. Neither position lessened the stiffness of his back nor the soreness of his tailbone. He glanced up at the chalkboard hanging beside the office's open door. The stage had been due at two that afternoon. It was now four. Again Vickery wished for a portion of Job's patience.

He looked up and down Sonora's single dusty street, wondering as he did about so many Texas towns just why anyone had been possessed to put up stakes there in the first place. From his position Vickery could clearly see the livery stable, where he had boarded his mount that morning. He supposed he should be grateful that his time in Sonora would be only a matter of hours rather than days.

Stretching out his legs, Vickery once again shifted on the bench. The new position felt no better than the last. He decided that part of his discomfort stemmed from the fact that he felt as naked as a babe without holster and cartridge belt, which were packed away in his black leather valise, tucked beneath the bench. Along with the holster was a change of clothing, Vickery's Ranger badge, and a bowie knife in a fringed-leather scabbard. The Texas Colt was now tucked beneath his belt on his back hip, concealed by his long black broadcloth coat.

"Reverend Vance?" A balding, middle-aged man appeared in the office door and addressed Vickery. "My wife, Thelma, just mixed up a pitcher of lemonade. Could I interest you in a glass?"

"Bless you, neighbor! That sounds as sweet as the milk and honey the good Lord promised the chosen people." Vickery started to rise, but the office manager waved him back to the bench.

"You sit there and rest yourself, and I'll bring you a glass." He stepped back into the office for the refreshment.

Vickery sighed with satisfaction. His undercover role as circuit preacher Jedediah Vance had him going to El Paso, where he was to perform a wedding service for a favorite niece. Since the sole purpose of the trip was the marriage and not spiritual ministry in towns scattered hither and yon, the Reverend Vance had decided on the luxury of a stagecoach over his usual four-legged conveyance.

"Here you go, Reverend," the office manager said, reappearing with two glasses of lemonade and handing one to Vickery. "You sure you wouldn't consider stayin' here in Sonora a few days? It's been a mighty long spell since we had us a God-fearin' Baptist preacher come to town. Most men of the cloth who pass through are Methodist. I ain't got nothin' against the Methodists, but when it comes to deliverin' a sermon, they always seem a mite weak-kneed. It takes a Baptist to put fire and spirit into the Good Word."

"Reckon I've always agreed with that sentiment," Vickery said sincerely after draining half the lemonade in one gulp. "I always thought it came from the way Methodists sprinkle a few drops of water on a soul's head and call that baptism. We've got to be fully immersed in the water to wash away our sins." He finished the glass with another swallow. "Mighty tasty lemonade. Tell your missus that it was greatly appreciated."

The office manager smiled, then looked up and nodded toward the east. "Looks like your waitin's about to end, Reverend. From the size of that dust cloud, I'd say that's the stage rollin' in."

Vickery turned and located a minor dust storm headed for town. "Hallelujah."

"Won't be but a few minutes to put a fresh team in the harness before she'll be headin' north for Eldorado," the stage manager said. "The stopover there'll be about three hours to allow everyone a rest and supper. By sunup you should be pullin' into San Angelo and Fort Concho. After that the route's pretty much westward all the way to El Paso."

Vickery nodded. "Sounds good to me. I'm anxious to get to my destination."

"You a horseman, Reverend Vance?" The question came from Bill House. House and his brother, Jake, who was doing his best to catch some shut-eye in the rocking coach, were ranchers from Las Cruces, a small town northwest of El Paso in the New Mexico Territory.

"Reckon I appreciate good horseflesh as well as the next man." Vickery sized up House. The rancher barely topped five-six, and beneath the wide-brimmed gray hat he wore was a head of thinning brown hair. He was about thirty. Jake was at least two years younger. Both men were solidly built; it would've been hard to find a spare ounce of fat on either of their well-muscled bodies.

"Horses, that's why me and Jake went to Arkansas. Morgans, specifically. Me and Jake bought us a Morgan mare and a stud. Gonna start breedin' Morgans. Bound to bring in some hard cash, wouldn't you say?"

"You got me there, neighbor," Vickery replied. "I've always preferred a range-bred horse. They got the endurance a man needs to cover a lot of open ground."

He only half-listened to House as the rancher began to extol the virtues of the Morgan breed, studying with sideways glances the other passengers packed into the Concord coach. Next to a napping Jake House was Leslie Wakefield, a pretty, delicate-looking spinster in her mid-twenties who called central Arkansas home. She was on her way to San Angelo to fill the position of second teacher in a new schoolhouse to be erected in the growing community.

Vickery found it difficult to imagine Leslie Wakefield as the murderer he sought. Still, he couldn't totally discard her. The killer who had butchered the four men and women was not a sane person. There was no way to correctly judge the insane. Often that insanity gave them uncanny strength.

The Ranger captain periodically nodded while Bill House continued to explain what he saw as the advantages of breeding Morgans, but Vickery's attention had moved from Leslie Wakefield to the last person crowded onto the seat, another man of the cloth, the Reverend Jacob Mason. The preacher was scarecrow thin to Vickery's eye. But Mason's deep, resonant voice carried strength in every syllable he uttered, and Vickery easily imagined him in the pulpit, his voice grabbing a congregation and holding them. Vickery had felt the strength of the preacher's handshake, too, and saw the determination in the man's dark-brown eyes. Mason had openly welcomed Jedediah Vance's company when Vickery climbed onto the stage, and for a full hour they had discussed sermons and congregations the way others might discuss sales figures or market prices. Mason appeared to be an open, good man.

The same could not be said about the man who sat across from the preacher. Wilson Cutter was a tinhorn gambler who made no attempt to disguise his profession. Vickery placed Cutter in his early thirties, of average height and build. The captain noted a bulge atop Cutter's right hip and an unnatural thickness under his left cuff. Had Vickery been a betting man, he would have placed a month's wages on the first bulge being a belly gun and the second a derringer.

Cutter, with his pomade-slick hair, had made no bones about why he was on the stage. "I ran into a spot of trouble on the Mississippi," he'd said. "Several riverboat captains made it clear that if they saw me again, the next time I went to sleep it'd be in a pine box. Since I'm a man who definitely enjoys life, I decided to travel west and try my luck at new gaming tables."

Luck, Vickery thought, probably never came into consideration when Cutter sat down at a poker table. It wasn't hard to imagine the man employing every devious holdout and bug ever devised. Unless Cutter was a lot better than the captain thought, the gambler wouldn't last long in this part of the country. Trail hands didn't appreciate being plucked like pigeons. A fast gun beat a fast off-the-bottom shuffle every day of the week.

Next to Cutter sat Lewis Jessup, a San Angelo rancher who Vickery placed in his late forties. The heavyset, gray-haired man looked worn and trail weary. Jessup said little to his fellow passengers. Except to mention that he was returning from visiting relatives in Arkansas, he'd kept quiet for the past hour. He sat staring into the night while he worked an unlit cigar between his teeth.

Beside Jessup sat another San Angelo rancher, Clayton Partee. The blond Partee was young, in his early twenties, and part of a new breed of Texas ranchers that was more than a little alien to Captain Vickery, who'd been raised among men who worked from sunup to sunset just to keep a roof over their families' heads and food on the table. The Ranger still found it hard to understand the cattle ranchers who'd suddenly arisen in the Lone Star State after the Civil War. These newcomers, out to make a fortune supplying meat to an eager nation, seemed more like greedy business tycoons than the ranchers Vickery had known all his life.

Partee's ranching interests apparently went beyond cattle. The young man was returning from Fort Smith, where he'd sold two hundred head of broken saddle stock to the U.S. Army. Partee bragged about the handsome profit he'd reaped from the transaction, money he'd invest in calves next spring.

Wedged against a window was Harry Farris. Like most of the stage's passengers, the dry-goods merchant's final destination was San Angelo. Vickery estimated the plump and balding man to be in his late thirties. Farris was returning from distant St. Louis, where he'd made arrangements to ship pianos and organs into Texas. Saying that new towns were popping up all over the western portion of the state, towns that had schools and churches, he had declared, "That means they'll need organs and pianos—and when they do, I'll be there to fill their needs."

Vickery found it difficult to seriously consider that Farris might be the killer he sought, but he couldn't rule him out any more than he could the schoolmarm.

He glanced up at the roof of the coach, envisioning the last coach passenger, who rode atop the stage with the luggage. Vickery recalled the soldier he had briefly met before boarding the stagecoach—a man not easy to forget. Tall and muscular, Lieutenant Jefferson Harper had seemed the epitome of the career Army officer in his smartly pressed uniform and with his erect bearing. Except that he was black.

While the cast of Jefferson's skin kept him from riding inside the stage with those of far lighter complexions, his color hadn't stopped the others from voicing what they knew of their fellow passenger.

"He is a West Point graduate," Leslie Wakefield had said, "and he has displayed nothing but the manners of an officer and a gentleman, no matter what his race."

"Uppity, if you ask me," Cutter had added. "Ever since the end of the war, they're all over the river—and all of 'em acting like something they're not."

Farris had nervously glanced at the roof and said softly, "He's to be the first Negro officer at Fort Concho. I can't help but wonder how the other soldiers will react to that. They're buffalo soldiers, you know? All of them just as black as the ace of spades. What will those soldiers do when they find out they got an officer who's one of their own kind?"

"Liable to rise up one night and slaughter every white officer in Fort Concho," Lewis Jessup had declared. "After that they'll likely swarm across the river into San Angelo and slit the throats of every man, woman, and child in town. They ain't nothin' but heathens. Little better than animals we saved from the jungle. Them damned Yankees never knew what they was doin' when they fought to set 'em free."

The passengers' comments were nothing new to Vickery. He'd heard them all before when Negro officers first came to Fort Davis in Texas's trans-Pecos region. The black officers there turned out to be no better or worse than their Caucasian counterparts, since, as was true with any race, the value of a man depended on that man himself. Which meant that until proven otherwise, he couldn't rule out Harper as a murderer.

Leslie Wakefield, Harry Farris, and Jacob Mason chose to take their supper inside the stage line's way station, along with the coach's driver and shotgun rider. Lieutenant Harper's decision was the same. However, his meal was served outside, behind the building.

The remaining passengers decided that liquid refreshment would make the hours remaining until the stage rolled into San Angelo far more bearable. Their choice of serving establishment was a one-room saloon called the Cactus Rose. Joking among themselves, they walked down Eldorado's single narrow street toward the saloon.

For the first time since boarding the stage Captain Vickery found himself caught in a knot tied by his own undercover story: The passengers remaining at the way station—except for Harper, about whom he knew close to nothing—sat at the bottom of his mental list of suspects; the others were going to a saloon, no fit place for the Reverend Jedediah Vance if Vickery intended to maintain his cover. But if he wanted to watch the others during the three-hour stopover in Eldorado, he couldn't remain in the way station.

"Reverend, will you take supper with us?" the stationmaster asked, pointing to a plate his wife had set for Vickery. "We'd be honored if you or Reverend Mason said grace over the meal. It's not often we have two men so close to God under our roof."

Ignoring the nagging hunger in his stomach, Vickery declined, saying, "You'll have to excuse me. I'm not accustomed to the rollin' and jostlin' of a stagecoach. I'm afraid my belly's actin' up on me a mite. I think what I need is a breath of cool evenin' air. If you'd set aside a couple pieces of cornbread and maybe a slice or two of that brisket for later—in case I get to feelin' better—I'd be awfully grateful."

The stationmaster nodded, and Vickery stepped outside and began casually strolling down the street. He had walked down and back the narrow avenue and begun to retrace his steps again by the time dusk darkened to a moonless night. Though the Reverend Jedediah Vance had no business inside the Cactus Rose, Vickery saw no harm in stationing himself across the street from the saloon, especially since a cluster of live oaks, with an inviting bench amid them, stood there. The trees' shadows would serve to veil him while he kept watch on the Cactus Rose's batwings. Ambling over to the bench, the Ranger settled down and waited.

No more than ten minutes had passed before he realized the impossible task he'd chosen for himself. New Mexico rancher Bill House left the saloon after time enough for only a quick beer. Vickery watched him start toward the way station on the edge of town but quickly lost him in the darkness. Ten minutes later Harry Farris, apparently having finished his meal at the way station, appeared out of the same darkness and walked into the Cactus Rose just as Wilson Cutter, who probably couldn't find enough players for a poker game, strolled out. Several minutes later Lieutenant Harper walked up and down the street twice. There seemed to be no purpose to his action other than to stretch his legs.

For an hour and a half the Ranger captain sat in the deep shadows watching the comings and goings of Eldorado's citizens while keeping an eye on the Cactus Rose. Fifteen minutes before the stage was due to pull out, the other passengers inside the saloon began to straggle out one at a time. None appeared to be any the worse for the beer and whiskey they had consumed.

Vickery rose and stretched. His plan had been fruitless. What worried him more, he thought as he slowly walked toward the way station, was how to handle the situation once he reached San Angelo. The final destination of all the passengers except the House brothers was the town forty miles to the north—and he himself was supposed to be going on to El Paso.

He felt as green as a pine sapling for having so hastily constructed his cover story about a niece's wedding. He tried appeasing himself, telling himself that, after all, this was the first time he'd ever worked undercover, that this assignment was a far cry from the Indian battles he'd fought in his younger days. It didn't help; he still felt foolish. He wondered if Cody, who worked undercover more often than not, ever painted himself into a corner with the stories he wove to hide his identity as a Ranger.

While deciding that he'd best wire ahead to Ranger headquarters in El Paso and tell them to keep an eye on the House brothers, Vickery found a solution to his predicament. Once in San Angelo he'd devise some twist to cover his continued presence in the town. The sickness of an old friend he'd say he visited nearby was the first thing that popped into mind—though he'd have to tread carefully there. Small towns, even those with an army fort, were notorious for everyone knowing everyone else's business. Once in San Angelo he'd reveal himself to the local sheriff and ask the man's help in piecing together a plausible story. Then he'd—

Vickery halted in midstride. He'd heard a cry. It was soft and muffled, but there was no mistaking it for anything else. Whether it had been male or female he couldn't discern, but the panic was unmistakable.

His pulse pounding, Vickery's head jerked from side to side, trying to locate the source of the sound. Nothing. He cocked his head and carefully listened.

There! He spun to the left. The crunch of stone beneath foot and the rustle of clothing came from a narrow alley running between a dry-goods shop and a feed store. Vickery pushed his coat back and freed the Texas Paterson Colt tucked under his belt. Gun drawn, he walked to the alley and peered in.

Vickery saw nothing but blackness. But someone was there. He was certain of it. He stepped a few feet into the alleyway, giving his eyes a few seconds to accustom themselves to the darkness. Then he cautiously continued farther in.

He was halfway down when he stumbled—over a body. Vickery dropped to a knee. His fingertips confirmed the vague image seen by his eyes: It was a woman, middle-aged, he believed. He touched her neck to read the throb of her pulse, then snatched his hand away. A warm and sticky substance flowed from the woman's neck. Blood. The woman's throat had been cut! In the few moments it had taken him to ascertain the direction of the cry and enter the alley, the killer had struck and a woman had died.

"Hellfire and damnation!" he spat.

His watch on the Cactus Rose had been useless. Nine people were too many for one man to keep under observation. Vickery thought of the few strides that separated trees from alley. He'd been so close to the man he sought, yet it was a lifetime away for the woman who lay crumpled at his feet. The butcher who'd done the dreadful deed couldn't have gone far, and Eldorado was too small a town to hide in.

Vickery got to his feet, thinking that the woman may not have died in vain. He had to move fast, get back to the way station. No person could commit such an act without managing to spill blood on himself. Vickery had to find that person before he had time to clean away the evidence.

A shadow moved within the shadows. Vickery sensed rather than saw something shifting to his right and started to turn toward it, his pistol aimed. But he wasn't quick enough. Something slammed into his head, sending out shock waves of pain, and blackness dropped like a curtain.

The killer stared down at the man and woman at his feet with an excited sense of triumph as he dropped the piece of two-by-four.

Two victims!

When the Reverend Jedediah Vance had joined the passengers in Sonora, the killer had viewed the presence of a man of the cloth as an omen, a signpost pointing away from his chosen path. But by offering himself so conveniently, Vance had proven the justification of the deeds.

Reaching into his jacket pocket, the killer eased the curved-bladed skinning knife from its leather sheath. He would have to work quickly tonight. The stagecoach wouldn't wait for anyone foolish enough to dally.

The killer knelt beside the woman whose throat lay open from ear to ear. First he would finish the task begun before Vance had appeared in the alley. Then the preacher would get the same treatment.

Leaning over the woman, the killer raised his knife and began his grisly task.

CHAPTER
|||||||||||||||||||||||||||||| **5** ||||||||||||||||||||||||||||

The taunting persistence of soft lips teasing his left ear woke Cody from a restful sleep. His eyes blinked open to a room filled with morning sunlight.

"The sleeper awakens," Marie Jermaine said playfully. She raised up on her elbow and smiled down into his face. "I was beginning to think that last night had drained away all your spirit."

Cody's smile answered the French beauty. She wiggled her naked body snugly against him; he lifted a hand and traced the curve of her cheek with a fingertip.

"Somehow I don't figure it's my spirit that concerns you right now," Cody said.

Marie captured his hand in hers. She lightly kissed his open palm. "Two weeks of absence cannot be filled in one night, Samuel."

Marie Jermaine was the only person who called him Samuel, everyone else calling him simply Cody—which he preferred—or, occasionally, Sam. But from the lips of this seductive redhead, Cody conceded to himself, he liked Samuel. In all honesty, he realized, even if Marie used his full handle of Samuel Clayton Woodbine Cody, he wouldn't have minded.

"And I suppose you reckon we should spend all of today lolling around here in this bed," he said. The thought had definite possibilities that Cody would've liked to explore, but he remembered that the rest of Company C was on patrol. He'd ride out to join them today—after he allowed himself the luxury of a few more moments with Marie, he told himself.

"In bed, yes"—Marie's eyes were filled with sensual light—"but lolling was not what I had in mind."

Cody wrapped an arm around her and effortlessly lifted her nakedness atop his own. Her stiff nipples threatened to dig holes in his chest. "It's downright sinful for any woman to look as beautiful as you do when the sun's just popped."

"You, *mon cher*, know just the right words to charm a woman's heart." Marie leaned close, and her lips softly brushed against Cody's as she spoke. "But sometimes a woman prefers deeds over words."

She gave a playful little wiggle, and Cody's reaction was amply evident. Delight flashed in Marie's eyes. "Ah! Ever you remain a man of action!"

With both arms encircling her satiny body, Cody drew her even closer. His mouth covered hers as their tongues—

Knuckles rapped sharply on the door.

"Cody?" Ernest Palmatier called from the corridor outside. "Sorry to bother you so early, Cody, but a telegram was just brought over. The messenger said to tell you it's Ranger business."

Groaning with disappointment, Cody looked at the voluptuous woman atop him and shrugged. Marie sighed and rolled off him and covered herself with a sheet.

Cody swung his legs over the side of the bed and grabbed his pants from the back of a chair. Slipping into the jeans, he crossed the room in two long strides and opened the door.

Ernest raised his eyebrows in apology as he handed the Ranger a neatly folded yellow paper. Keeping his eyes discreetly diverted from the room's interior, the hotelier said, "I hope it is not bad news."

"So do I," Cody replied. Nodding, he closed the door, then unfolded the wire and read silently, his face darkening as he did so. He glanced up at Marie and said, "So much for hoping."

"What is it, *mon cher*?"

"It's Cap'n Vickery." Cody stepped to the wardrobe and pulled out a clean work shirt. "He's been hurt." He tossed the telegram to the bed.

"May I?" Marie picked up the wire when Cody nodded and read aloud: " 'To Texas Ranger Company C Del Rio. Captain Wallace Vickery attacked here last night. Injured but alive and recovering. Sheriff Sean MacArt, Eldorado.' Samuel, this does not provide much information," she noted, worry lines creasing her fair forehead.

"That's what's got me bothered." Bothered more than Cody was willing to say. He remembered the two-page telegram from Major Jones on Vickery's desk. Odds were the captain had run head-on into the brutal killer he'd ridden after—coming out on the short end of that meeting. "There's nobody over at headquarters. That leaves me to ride north and see what's up." He buttoned his shirt and tucked it into his pants, pulled on his vest, then grabbed his holster and gun belt from the bedpost, where he always hung them.

"I understand, Samuel." Marie tried unsuccessfully to hide the disappointment in her voice.

Cody walked to the edge of the bed and leaned down, giving her a long passionate kiss. "We'll make it up to each other when I get back," he said when their lips had finally parted. "I promise you that."

Marie smiled. "That is a promise on which I intend to collect."

He kissed her again, lightly this time. "I don't welsh on promises—especially to beautiful women."

"As I said, you have a way of saying the right thing, Samuel . . . even if it is the wrong time."

When Cody entered the Eldorado sheriff's office, the man behind the cluttered desk stood and sized up the trail-weary stranger in a single glance that ended by alighting on his silver badge.

"You that Ranger Sam Cody who answered my wire to Del Rio?"

"I'm Cody," the Ranger confirmed.

"And I'm Sean MacArt."

As tall as Cody, the sheriff had at least twenty pounds on the Ranger, none of which appeared to be fat. Cody stuck out a hand, which MacArt shook in a grip that left Cody's knuckles aching. He was glad they were on the same side of the law.

"How's Cap'n Vickery doing? Your telegram said he'd been attacked and injured," Cody said.

MacArt gave an embarrassed snigger. "To tell the truth, I thought your captain was a dead man when I wired you. Turned out he looked a hell of a lot worse than he actually was. The widow Lancaster's been seein' after him. To my way of thinkin', he looks like he could be up and about, if the widow gives her okay."

Cody's eyebrow rose skeptically. "If the widow gives her okay? What about the town doctor?"

MacArt shrugged. "Ain't nigh enough folks hereabouts to keep a medico in town. If things are serious enough, a body's got to ride to San Angelo to get a doctor to look him over. Anything else, Mary Lou Lancaster handles. She's got savvy when it comes to potions and poultices. Don't worry none about Captain Vickery. He's been in good hands." He grinned. "And if your captain ain't spoken for, he's probably gotten even better lookin' after, seein' as how he's just about the right age for Mary Lou, who's been without a husband for two years."

Cody repressed a chuckle. In the years he'd known Wallace Vickery, he'd never imagined him in the company of a woman, having always thought of Vickery as a confirmed bachelor. Besides, Cody found it difficult to picture a woman attracted to a man of the captain's temperament. To begin with, she'd have to be part grizzly bear. . . .

"I'll walk you over to the Lancaster place, if you want," Sheriff MacArt suggested.

"I'd appreciate that."

The two lawmen left the office and walked up Eldorado's main street. Except for a handful of womenfolk looking at items displayed in a couple of shop windows, there were few signs of life.

"It stays this way here most of the time," the sheriff explained. " 'Cept come Saturday nights when cowhands ride in from twenty miles 'round. The Cactus Rose over yonder can do a month's worth of business some Saturday nights. For the most part my job's to keep the rowdies in line. Occasionally one of the cowboys might get it in his head to try to throw down on someone. Then I've got to do some head knockin'.''

Cody nodded knowingly. Before taking the Ranger's oath, he'd worn a sheriff's badge in El Paso. A town lawman's duty mostly consisted of strolling up and down the streets, making the citizenry feel secure. Saturday nights, however, could be another story. Sometimes if a man wasn't handy with his fists and quick with a gun, he didn't live to see Sunday morning.

"This Captain Vickery of yours claims to be a man of the cloth as well as a Ranger." MacArt's statement was tinged with surprise.

"Preaches up fire and brimstone when asked to," Cody confirmed. "Not in any regular way anymore—he sometimes fills in for one of the local preachers if they've taken sick or are off visiting relatives—and he's a handy man to have around if there's need of a marriage. Or a funeral."

The sheriff chuckled. "Damnedest preacher I've ever run into. Not only does he carry a pistol and a star, but he acts as ornery as a Spanish mule. Don't believe I've heard him speak a word in what a man could call a normal tone of voice. He kinda growls. Even when I was tryin' to carry him over to Widow Lancaster's to get him seen after, he was a-growlin' at me."

Cody echoed his fellow lawman's chuckle.

After walking another block, MacArt gestured at a whitewashed house with green trim. They crossed the neat yard to a spacious porch that wrapped around three sides of the structure, and MacArt knocked on the door.

A plump woman with gold-rimmed spectacles perched on the end of her nose and snow-white hair braided in a tight bun answered the door. Her round face brightened with a wide smile when she saw the sheriff. "Come to call on my patient, Sheriff MacArt?"

"Yes, ma'am. We'd like to talk with Captain Vickery for a piece, if we wouldn't be puttin' you out none." MacArt took off his hat and nodded at the man beside him. "This here's Sam Cody. He's ridden all the way up from Del Rio to see the captain."

"Mr. Cody"—the widow smiled at the Ranger—"I'm pleased to make your acquaintance. Won't you come on in? Wallace is in the back bedroom. It gets full sun in the afternoon as well as the southern breeze."

"Thank you, ma'am." Cody removed his own Stetson as he stepped over the threshold and followed Mrs. Lancaster into the house and down a narrow hallway. He hadn't missed the woman's reference to "Wallace." It was one of the few times he'd ever heard anyone call Vickery by anything other than "Captain."

"Wallace?" The woman stopped at a closed door on the left. She rapped lightly. "Wallace, are you awake? Two gentlemen are here to see you."

"'Gentlemen'?" Vickery's gravelly voice answered. "Mrs. Lancaster, I don't know no gentlemen. The last one I met was President Sam Houston."

"It's Sheriff MacArt and a Ranger friend of yours," the widow replied with all the patience in the world. "They'd like to visit with you for a few minutes."

"Ranger? Dabnabbit, woman, why didn't you say that in the first place? Send 'em on in."

Cody smiled to himself. Vickery sounded none the worse for wear. And he didn't appear to be ailing any when Mrs. Lancaster opened the door to reveal him sitting up in a brass bed with a newspaper spread around him. A tray with a pot of coffee and a plate heaped with doughnuts sat on a table beside the bed. Vickery held a half-eaten doughnut in one hand.

"Cody!" Captain Vickery's eyes widened when the Ranger stepped into the bedroom. "I'd never reckoned Whitcomb sendin' you along."

Before Cody could explain, Mrs. Lancaster interrupted. "Sheriff MacArt, Mr. Cody, would either of you like some coffee? I just made a fresh pot for Wallace. I'm sure he wouldn't mind sharing it."

"No, thank you, ma'am," Cody replied, while the sheriff shook his head.

"What about you, Wallace?" The widow stepped beside the bed and had the captain lean forward so she could fluff the pillows behind his back. "Is there anything else I can get for you? I still have some of those sugar cookies left over from yesterday. Would you like a few of those to go with your coffee?"

Cody stroked his mustache with a large hand to hide his grin. For a fleeting instant he saw an expression of complete contentment pass across Vickery's face. The captain was reveling in the widow's attention. But when he spoke, his voice was its usual deep gruffness.

"Madam, I have want for nothing, except for a little privacy to talk with these men. We've the law to discuss, and our topic is not suitable for the ears of a gentlewoman such as yourself. Now, if you'd excuse us . . . ?"

"Of course." The widow's eyes fluttered shyly, and she hurried toward the bedroom door. As she closed it behind her she added softly, "But remember, Wallace, this is a very small town. Everyone knows how Emma Pilcher was killed."

Vickery sighed with exasperation as he turned to Cody and the sheriff. "That's as fine a God-fearing woman as ever walked the face of this earth, but sometimes she's enough to try the patience of a saint—"

Cody laughed to himself. The captain, for all his Biblical invocation, fell far short of being a saint.

"—and she hovers over a man like a mother hen. It's enough to smother a soul." Vickery then grinned and winked at his visitors. "But when it comes to cookin', a man couldn't ask for better. My, how that woman can cook!" His face became serious. "Never thought Whitcomb'd send you up here, Cody," he repeated.

"He didn't. I was the only one at headquarters." The Ranger gave a thumbnail report on his encounter with the rustlers near Eagle Pass and his return to Del Rio. Leaving out mention of his night with Marie, he concluded, "I was about to ride out and try to join the company when I received Sheriff MacArt's wire. I came immediately."

Vickery's cheeks flushed. He concealed his chagrin

behind a gruff cough. "Afraid I bit off a mite more than one man could chew and went walkin' into a yellow jacket's nest."

The captain detailed all that had occurred since he'd left Del Rio, including his impressions of the nine passengers on the stagecoach. He then recounted how he found the body and was knocked unconscious by the killer.

"This ain't no run-of-the-mill owlhoot we're dealin' with," Vickery said. "Whoever's killin' these folks got a streak of meanness running through him that's a mile or three wide. And he keeps it hidden real well." He turned to MacArt and asked, "Would you say that's about right, Sheriff?"

"Meanness don't rightly describe what I found in that alley," MacArt said somberly. "Meanness is a hardheaded cowpuncher determined to bust a few heads just 'cause he took a notion to bust heads. I never saw nothin' like what I found in that alley. Never!"

MacArt paused to pull a tobacco pouch and a brier pipe from a pocket. He filled and lit the pipe, blowing a thin stream of blue smoke into the air. "I was makin' my early evenin' rounds when I heard this low, kinda deranged chucklin' comin' from the alleyway." He shook his head slowly. "I ain't the kind of fella gets the jitters easy, but this sound . . ." The sheriff paused and drew on the pipe, holding the smoke a moment before releasing it in a swirling cloud.

Cody studied the lawman's face. Whatever he was dredging up was clearly something that he'd have preferred to allow to sleep.

MacArt looked at the two Rangers. "Whoever was doin' that laughin' must've heard me comin', 'cause the next thing I heard was the sound of someone runnin' away. I lit out after whoever it was and damned near broke my neck when I fell over the captain, who was bleedin' and moanin'." He paused again. "And then I found Emma Pilcher. It took only a brush of my hand on her cold skin to know she was dead. But I didn't know how dead until me and my deputy carried her out into the light."

Cody considered that he had seen the worst one man can do to another. He was wrong. He was sickened as MacArt detailed the grisly, bloody work the killer had performed on Emma Pilcher.

"He apparently started out the way he did on Captain Vickery. He used a blade to carve shallow crosshatches into her chest and bosoms," MacArt said.

To emphasize the sheriff's description, Vickery pulled down the coverlet and pulled up his nightshirt, displaying his chest—which was etched from neck to midriff with a series of thin crisscrossed cuts. There was an almost artistic precision to the way the killer had worked his blade.

"The cuts got deeper the lower he worked," MacArt continued. "Finally he dressed her, just like a hunter'd dress a deer or an antelope. I never saw nothin' like it. Emma didn't look human no more. She looked more like a piece of meat ready for the smokehouse."

"I was lucky," Vickery said. "Like as not I'd have ended up the same way if the sheriff hadn't come along."

Cody turned to the window and drew in a deep breath of the cool afternoon breeze, trying to rid his mind of the almost perceptible smell of offal. He now understood MacArt's earlier discomfort. It wasn't easy for a man, no matter how hardened, to talk about such butchery.

After several puffs on the pipe the sheriff added, "Still worse—if you can imagine that somethin' could be worse—was that Emma's ears were missing. They'd been cut from her head."

"Her ears?" Cody stared at the town's lawman.

Vickery cleared his throat. "I had the sheriff here send a few wires out for me, checkin' in the other towns where the killer struck. The ears were missin' from the bodies there, too."

"That bastard!" Cody spat. "It's like he's cutting off the ears like a hunter takes a buck's antlers, as a trophy."

"Or a Comanch takin' a scalp," Vickery added.

Blowing another cloud of smoke toward the ceiling, MacArt said, "Them other sheriffs gave me a description of their victims. They was sliced up same as Emma."

"He—or she—likes what he's doing," Vickery said. "He

enjoys it the way some shootists like to cut other men down."

The captain had voiced Cody's thoughts. It seemed that the killer found some type of depraved pleasure in the murders. A man didn't go to so much—

The Ranger's thoughts stumbled when he realized what Vickery had said. "He or *she*? Cap'n, you don't think a woman could do this, do you?"

"Don't reckon we know for sure, son," Vickery replied. "I didn't get a real look at the killer, just a vague impression of someone standin' in the shadows. So I can't say for certain if it's a man or a woman." He looked at MacArt. "What do you think, Sheriff?"

"My instincts say it's a man—'cept like you, Captain, I didn't really see anybody, so I can't rule out a woman." MacArt shook his head angrily. "I sure wasn't playin' it smart. I never thought about the stage or the fact that a murderer could be on it. While my deputy and me was carryin' Emma out of the alley, I let that son of a bitch roll right out of town. It's a bitter pill to swallow. I'd have the bastard that done this if I'd stopped the stage. I just wasn't thinkin'."

Cody felt sorry for MacArt. That kind of mistake was hard to live with. If the stage *had* been stopped, the killer would be in Eldorado that very moment. Exactly which one of the passengers it was might not yet be known, but at least they'd be able to keep an eye on everyone.

Trying to bolster the lawman's spirits, Cody said, "It was finding the body of a woman you knew butchered that way. That would've gotten to any of us. Something like that catches a man off guard."

MacArt nodded, but it was easy to see that the Ranger's words did little to help. He took the pipe from between his teeth and studied the bowl. It had gone out. He looked up again, at Cody.

"I followed Captain Vickery's suggestion and wired ahead to the other town sheriffs on the stage's route, warnin' them about possible trouble comin' their way. It made sense to prepare 'em."

"Did you send a wire to San Angelo?" Cody asked, recalling that most of the stage's passengers were headed there.

"I sure did."

Cody nodded. The telegrams were a good move. Should the killer strike again, the local lawmen would be forewarned and ready to take action. Hopefully. Cody was willing to bet the killer's destination had been San Angelo. That was the place to pick up the trail again.

The Ranger stared out the bedroom's open window at Mrs. Lancaster's well-kept garden behind the house. The scene was beautiful and tranquil, a stark contrast to what the killer left in his wake.

"You know, the killer might not be on the stage," Cody suggested as he turned from the window. "Could be it's somebody *trailing* the stage. Fact is, the killings are so crazy that it could be anyone."

"I thought of that, but the sheriff and his deputy have kept an eye peeled for any strangers in town, and they've come up with nothin'," Vickery replied as he threw back the covers and swung his legs over the side of the bed.

Cody stared at the captain. "What do you think you're doing?"

"Goldurnit, what does it *look* like I'm doin'? I'm gettin' out of this bed." Vickery's eyes narrowed as he returned Cody's stare. "You and me are goin' after a killer."

Cody held up his hands. "Hold on a minute, Cap'n. Rank or no rank, you aren't riding anywhere until Mrs. Lancaster gives the okay. You're healing up well, but it won't do any good to have an injured man in the saddle. Besides, my mount needs a rest after two and a half days on the trail. A night in a stall with good grain and hay will have him ready for the ride to San Angelo in the morning."

He paused and pointed at the plate of doughnuts. "You aren't going to be eating high on the hog between here and San Angelo. A couple more of Mrs. Lancaster's meals and another good night's rest will help bring back your strength."

Cody could virtually see the blustery reply dancing on the tip of Vickery's tongue, but a glance at the sugary doughnuts had the captain swallowing back his words. "Reckon you're right about your horse. He needs his rest. But no matter what the widow says, you and me ride north tomorrow mornin'. Is that understood?"

"Understood."

"Good. 'Cause we're goin' to bring that madman in for a proper hangin'—even if we've got to follow him to hell and back."

CHAPTER
||||||||||||||||||||||||||| **6** |||||||||||||||||||||||||||||

Restless dreams woke the killer from a shallow sleep. Sweat poured from his body to drench the bed sheets.

The hunger had returned.

No, it was wrong! It was horribly wrong! A flash of sanity pushed through the madness, reaching his consciousness. The hunger had to be challenged. He had turned away from it those many years ago; he could turn away again.

The hunger gnawed.

Twisting fitfully in the bed, the killer lay facing the open window, silently beseeching the cool breeze blowing in to clear the cobwebs from his head. The plea went unanswered. Confusion and torment reigned. The killer flopped to his back and clamped his eyes shut, mouthing all the prayers learned in a lifetime.

The hunger ate deep, demanding to be sated.

No! The killer's hands balled into tortured fists. No! This was so wrong. He knew that. Underneath the madness he knew that.

The hunger screamed out to be fulfilled.

Warmth reached his body . . . and the feel of flesh touching flesh. He looked over at his sleeping companion. It would be so easy to sate the hunger, to—

No, not here! This was home. He had to be careful. Those he chose must not be connected to him in any way.

Reason prevailed. He shifted, breaking the contact with the warm body beside him. Best to try to sleep again.

The hunger wailed like a raging storm. It throbbed, a low ache that grew into a pounding pain.

Slipping from the bed, alert for the slightest sound indicating that his companion had awakened, the killer got dressed in clothing as black as the night outside. He paused for a moment at the bedroom door and listened again. All was still. On tiptoes the killer stole down the hallway and hurried from the house.

The night air seemed to change around him. What had been cool and refreshing but seconds ago now felt torrid and intense. Any thoughts of danger, of being caught, faded.

A soft whistling, a tune barely recognizable as "Buffalo Gals," swung the killer around. Across a narrow dirt street, walking beneath the mesquite trees that lined the lane, was a boy, no more than ten years old. He moved purposefully, unaware of the eyes that followed his each and every step.

The hunger flared. A child! There was so much life in a child! How exciting to end so much life! The killer slipped the curved knife from its sheath and ran a fingertip along the blade.

Like a mountain lion stalking its prey, he darted across the street, then crept through the mesquites' shadows, hanging back a hundred feet. There was no need to rush. The hunger guided him; it would tell him when to act.

For three blocks the killer trailed the child, steadily closing the gap between them until they were but fifty feet apart. Then the boy abruptly turned into a yard, skipped up the porch steps, and knocked on the door. Within minutes a light flared at a front window, and then the door opened.

"Tommy, what are you doing out so late? Is anything wrong?" the man standing in the doorway asked.

"It's my ma, Doc," the boy answered. "Pa sent me here to fetch you to our house. He said Ma's ready to bring me a brother."

Smiling, the physician reached out and ushered the boy inside. "Is she, now? Well, you come wait in the parlor while I get dressed. Then we'll drive back to your house in my carriage."

The door closed, and the killer stood alone in the night, staring forlornly at the house. Now he had to find another one marked for the blade.

But it wouldn't be here. Not in San Angelo's sleeping residential district. He must go where men and women reveled in the night.

With determined strides the killer hurried down the street, turning when he reached the corner. Ahead, where lights glared from saloons and cantinas, men, many with soiled doves on their arms, strolled up and down the town's main street. Across the Concho River twinkled the lights of the Army fort with its black-skinned buffalo soldiers. But the killer didn't have to wade across the river. The chosen one would be found in San Angelo proper. He was certain of it.

The hunger propelled the killer to an alley that gaped between a barbershop and a saddlery. Squatting between two wooden barrels filled with leather scraps, he waited.

A buggy trundled down the street, stopping before a house known for the ladies of the night who kept rooms within. From the buggy stepped a man in a three-piece suit with a long black cigar clenched between his teeth. The killer recognized the suited man as San Angelo's acting mayor. The elected mayor had been gunned down in a barroom fight two months before.

The sheriff, tin star pinned to his plaid shirt, approached the buggy. The lawman tipped his hat to the acting mayor, then walked on, allowing the city official to enter the house and feed his depraved desires.

Soldiers, pockets heavy with their monthly pay, moved up and down the street in small packs, wandering from saloon to saloon. By the coming morning those pockets would be empty, and the town's purveyors of filth would have grown richer.

Twice soldiers exited a saloon across the street and crossed over into the alley to relieve themselves against a wall. Both men stood less than fifteen feet from the killer but never noticed the shadow-within-the-shadows that watched them. He crouched silently and let them pass. The time was not right. They were not right.

An hour, then two, crawled by, and still the killer waited for the hunger to guide the skinning knife to the one chosen for this night. Beyond the mouth of the alley the street grew gradually quiet. Here and there lights winked out in cantinas and cathouses. No longer did buggies roll past the alley. Now only an occasional horseman rode by, or a pair of men staggered from swinging batwings to help each other on their walk home. The killer remained crouched between the barrels, hand in his pocket caressing the skinning knife, waiting. Patiently waiting.

The yellow glow of oil lamps burned in only two of the town's saloons when the cowboy strode outside. His head bobbled unsteadily from side to side, as if he was seeking company in his night of alcoholic revelry. Finding the streets all but barren, he blurted a curse damning San Angelo for its inability to satisfy him. He leaned against a hitching post, and after three attempts he managed to roll himself a cigarette. It took only two matches to light the smoke. A pleased grin spread across his face when he exhaled.

The cowhand peered up the street and then down as if uncertain what course to take next. After due consideration—and several moments of leg crossing—his gaze turned to the alley directly in front of him. He drew another drag from the cigarette and stumbled forward.

The killer tensed. The time had come. His hand tightened around the sheathed haft of the knife, and he slowly withdrew the weapon from his coat pocket.

The killer stood and stepped away from the barrels when the cowboy entered the alley and began to fiddle with his trouser buttons. The sound of movement brought the cowhand's head around, and he blinked several times, trying to clear the alcoholic haze.

The killer struck. Not with the knife's blade, but with the heavy horn haft, driving it like a sledgehammer into the cowboy's temple and sending him hurling against the barbershop wall. With a groan, he slid down the building to come to rest on his backside.

For a moment the killer stood in a wide-legged stance above the fallen man, waiting. But the cowboy didn't rise.

The blow had knocked him out. Reaching down with his left hand, the killer grabbed the cowboy's collar and dragged him down to his back. Unsheathing the blade, the killer sliced the cowboy's shirt from his body; then he cut away his pants and pulled off his boots until the cowboy lay stark naked in the dirt, his chest rising and falling in a steady rhythm as though he merely slept.

Good! A familiar gloating filled the killer's own chest. This one still lived. It was always better when they lived.

The hunger burned brightly within him now. The earlier doubts, the struggle to deny his destiny, seemed so distant. He had let the hunger act as a guide and once again it had proven itself. Hadn't the hunger guided him to this alley and told him to wait until the time was right?

And now the time was definitely right!

The killer straddled the cowhand and leaned over him. With the very tip of the skinning knife he began to carve crosshatches into his victim's chest, and black blood oozed from the wounds. As always, the killer thought how much the cuts resembled the crisscrossed welts left on his own body by his stepfather's punishing hickory stick.

Cody glanced surreptitiously at Captain Vickery as they reached the outskirts of San Angelo. Though the captain had never complained during the forty-mile ride and had, in fact, insisted he was as fit as a fiddle, Cody could see the weariness etched on his face. Still, Vickery had never protested the lengthy rests Cody had insisted they take "for the horses" and had always been perfectly willing to find a piece of shade and stretch out for a cat-nap.

Mrs. Lancaster had explained that while the knife wounds weren't deep, Vickery had suffered considerable loss of blood, and she estimated it would take a full week before the Ranger captain was up to his old strength. She had instructed Cody to see that Vickery ate a lot of red meat.

"That'll help bring his blood back," she had explained. "And I know he's got a taste for sweets, but vegetables will do him more good. Greens especially."

Finding red meat on the trail wasn't always easy, though Cody had managed to bring down an antelope about ten miles north of Eldorado. But the only greens he'd been able to find were dandelions, which he boiled up. Vickery had taken one bite and then tossed them aside, staring at Cody as though his fellow Ranger had gone unexpectedly mad.

Cody had understood the captain's reaction when he tasted the greens himself. They'd been bitter beyond belief. "My ma fixes them up just fine," he'd said by way of apology. "Reckon I never paid enough attention to how she does it."

"Best leave your ma's cookin' to your ma," Vickery had grunted, going back to chewing on a piece of the antelope meat.

Well, Cody thought as they entered San Angelo, *at least Vickery'll be able to get the fare he needs here.* One of the few pleasant recollections the Ranger had of his last visit to this town, located on the confluence of the three branches of the Concho River, was that he'd eaten well. That was about the only good thing he could say about the wide-open town.

The water flowing in the Concho's three branches had first brought Mexican settlers to this dry, hot land, but the fierce Comanche and their constant raids from out of the high plains had kept the town from being any more than a village for decades. Then along came the U.S. Army. They chose the site for a fort for the same reason the Mexican farmers had settled the land: water—a precious commodity in a land just a few inches of rainfall away from being called a desert.

Fort Concho with its Negro soldiers—buffalo soldiers, as the Comanche called them—was largely responsible for the defeat of the Comanche raiders. The fort was also in large measure the reason for the town's wild ways, Cody knew. For wherever there were soldiers, there were those only too happy to devise ways to relieve them of their monthly pay. Gamblers, saloon owners, and prostitutes flocked to the small town, all willing to provide the services required to sate the desires of the soldiers. It didn't matter what color their skin was; what mattered was the color of the money in their pockets.

As he and Vickery led their mounts toward the heart of town, Cody was certain of one thing about San Angelo: He was glad he wasn't its sheriff. *Every* night was Saturday night here. Sheriffing became a job in which laws were overlooked rather than enforced.

"Cody, you got a preference as to where we hang our hats?" Vickery asked.

"Whatever strikes your fancy," Cody answered. In truth, he'd forgotten the name of the hotel he'd stayed in during his last visit. But he remembered the flea bites.

Vickery nodded to the left. "Over yonder looks good. Leastwise, it appears new enough it might still be clean."

Newness was as good a measure for selecting a hotel as any other he could think of, Cody told himself. The captain's choice, a two-story structure with a blue-and-white sign proclaiming it to be the Three Rivers One Hotel, did appear relatively new. The yellow pine siding still retained its original color, although dark streaks stained the wood around each nail, indicating that the building had weathered more than one rainstorm.

"There's a livery stable up the street," Vickery said, pointing as he dismounted in front of the hotel. "You go take care of the horses, and I'll go in and get us rooms. I'll be in the saloon when you get back—seein' about gettin' myself some dinner that don't include dandelion greens."

Cody took the captain's reins and continued along the street. Something told him that he'd forever regret his attempt at providing the healthy food Mrs. Lancaster had suggested. He felt certain that Vickery wouldn't forget the dandelions for a long time—or let his fellow Ranger forget, either.

Reaching the livery stable, Cody dismounted and was met by an unshaven man in manure-stained overalls. The man gestured to five empty stalls at the back of his stable and said, "The price is seventy-five cents a day per stall; a dollar if you want me to feed my own grain. The stalls are mucked mornin' and afternoon, and I water mornin', noon, and night."

"A dollar a horse?" Cody was astonished. That was four times what a man would pay to board a horse in any other

Texas town. Except Austin, the capital seat. Folks there learned quickly from politicians and would gouge a man at each and every opportunity.

"Only seventy-five cents if you feed your own grain," the stableman answered, apparently finding nothing unusual about his price.

Digging into a pocket, Cody came up with two silver dollars and flipped them to the owner. "Don't know how long I'll be in town. I'll see to my bill day by day."

The man took the horses and led them toward their stalls as the Ranger turned and walked back toward the Three Rivers One.

San Angelo gave no indication of slowing down despite the setting sun. If anything the opposite was true. Cody studied the increased traffic with a professional eye. Sun-bonneted housewives and matrons no longer graced the wooden sidewalks; the women sauntering by or posing in doorways or leaning from second-story windows wore heavily painted faces and revealing dresses. Their queries to passing men were explicit and daring.

The makeup of the men had also changed. Businessmen dressed in black suits gradually disappeared, and army blue became the predominant color. With the day's duties done, buffalo soldiers from Fort Concho found their way across the river to seek the pleasures of the evening. They were joined by the ranch hands hitching their mounts outside their favorite watering hole or accepting the offers of the painted ladies cajoling them.

Cody entered the Three Rivers One Hotel lobby, which consisted of a small desk and three straight-backed wooden chairs, thankful that he'd hidden his badge in his watch. To wear a Ranger badge in San Angelo seemed tantamount to pinning a target to one's chest and inviting any half-drunk cowboy or soldier to take a potshot at it. A weary-looking desk clerk pointed Cody toward batwing doors to the left.

"Your friend said you was to find him in the saloon. Whiskey and food are served in the same room here in the Three Rivers."

Thanking the clerk, the Ranger stepped into an immense room that covered at least three-quarters of the hotel's bottom floor. The size of the saloon left little doubt that the Three Rivers' proprietor made the majority of his profit from the sale of rotgut rather than the rental of rooms. The hour might be early, but at least thirty patrons had found their way to the bar or sat around tables.

It was at one of these tables, near a pair of glass-windowed doors leading to the street, that Cody found Captain Vickery. He arrived in time to hear a waiter standing beside Vickery sputter, "Cider? You want a glass of *cider*?"

Vickery gave the waiter a glare that had made more than one Ranger tremble with apprehension. "I don't believe I mumbled. And you don't appear deaf. I said I want a glass of cider."

Cody caught the glances of several of the saloon's patrons—all focused on Vickery—while he walked toward the captain's table. Del Rio's saloonkeepers usually kept a jug of apple cider stored under their bars in case Vickery happened to pay them an unexpected visit. That Vickery generally shunned alcohol didn't bother them. They were honored when the Ranger captain entered their doors and ordered a glass of cider.

"We ain't got no cider," the waiter said, shaking his head and shooting a grin to a heavyset man standing behind the bar.

"Then what about sarsaparilla? I've been known to drink a bottle of that on occasion." Vickery's voice deepened as he said slowly and distinctly, "You do have sarsaparilla, don't you?"

The waiter glanced at the bartender, who shook his head, then looked back at Vickery. "No sarsaparilla, but we might have a touch of mornin' milk, if that suits your taste."

Vickery's face turned an angry shade of crimson. "Is there something wrong with your eyes? Do I look like some dadblamed infant? If I'd wanted milk, I'd've asked you for it. If you ain't got cider or sarsaparilla, then bring me a cup of coffee. That is, if gettin' a man a cup of coffee won't strain your back!"

"Coffee it is," the waiter answered as Cody joined the captain at the table. "So, let's see, that's a steak, rare, with potatoes and onions and a cup of coffee." The waiter then looked at Cody for his order.

"I'll have the same," the Ranger answered. "But make my steak well done."

"Okay, that's one rare steak and one—"

The waiter wasn't given the chance to complete his sentence. A lean-looking ranch hand, dressed in worn chaps and spurs, turned from the bar and called out, "Them two don't look like they got the money for a man's drink, Smitty. Why don't you bring 'em a beer? Me and Tate and Willie here will foot the bill."

Before Cody could respond, Vickery shifted in his chair, eyeing the three cowboys who stared at him from the bar, and called, "That's a generous offer, neighbor, and I thank you kindly, but coffee'll be just fine."

As the captain turned back around, the three cowhands glanced at one another and moved away from the bar. Cody's eyes narrowed. Vickery's reply left him baffled. Didn't he know these three weren't acting neighborly? Had it been that long since the captain had walked into a saloon outside of Del Rio that he no longer recognized an invitation to trouble?

The three men advanced across the room, stopping directly behind Vickery. Each held a half-drained beer mug in his hand. The thick dust that covered their clothing was testimony to the distance they'd ridden to reach the saloon.

"Jeb, I don't think this old coot understood ya," one of the men said in a slightly slurred voice that spoke of at least three other beers preceding the one in his hand. "Maybe you should make yourself clearer. Could be Grandpa here ain't hearin' so good no more."

"Willie, I don't think *you* understand. This dried-out old buzzard heard every word I said," the cowboy called Jeb said with a mocking sneer. "He ain't deaf; he just don't like our company. Or maybe our beer ain't good enough for him."

Cody's spine drummed out a warning. These three had worked up a streak of meanness somewhere on the trail and saw the captain as an easy target to work it out of their systems. There was no way around it. They were spoiling for a fight—as long as they picked a fight they felt certain they could win. Three to two were good odds, especially when one of the two was sporting the white hair of advancing age.

The tall Ranger's right hand dropped to the Frontier Colt holstered on his hip. If it took a gun to make certain Vickery wasn't hurt, then so be it.

But before he could act, Vickery spoke up, without looking at the threesome. "Friend, I'm not out to insult no one. If it's a drink you'd like me to share with you, then you're welcome to pull up a chair and have a cup of coffee."

The cowhands laughed. Jeb spoke again. "Coffee's somethin' a man drinks when he can't wrap his hand 'round a glass of beer. You ain't one of them teetotaler Baptists, now, are you? One of them folks that thinks a man who drinks hisself a little beer is goin' straight to the fires of hell?"

Jeb held his half-filled mug over Vickery's head. With a wink at his two companions, he slowly began to tilt the glass, intent on dowsing the captain with its contents.

Whether Vickery saw the flicker of Cody's eyes or had a third eye in the back of his head Cody didn't know, but the captain abruptly stiffened and growled in a stone-cold voice, "Friend, the last person that gave me a bath was my saintly mother, may she rest in the arms of the Lord. Even then folks tell I yelled and fought like a wildcat. I'd give it two thinks before I downturned that glass."

The mischievous meanness in Jeb's eyes turned to anger. "Why, you old bastard! Before we're through with you, you'll be lapping beer off the floor like some—"

The cowboy's words ended in a startled cry. Without warning, Vickery shoved from his chair. In what appeared to be a clumsy movement, his shoulder struck Jeb's glass hard and sent the contents hurling into the cowboy's face.

Vickery turned and sputtered, "Why, friend. I'm terribly sorry! Here, let me buy *you* a drink."

With an uncanny speed and certainty that left Cody staring wide-eyed, the captain's left hand snaked out and grabbed Jeb's mug. He wrenched it away from the cowhand with such force that the mug slammed back into the side of Willie's temple. For an instant Willie swayed with a bewildered expression on his face; then he collapsed to the saloon floor, unconscious.

"Oh, my! Now look what I went and did." Vickery dropped the beer mug beside Willie as he continued his oafish act. "Would you two look at that! I knocked out your friend. Don't you think you should give him a hand?"

This time both of the captain's arms shot out. His meaty hands grabbed the ranch hands by the necks of their shirts and jerked them toward the fallen Willie. The expert maneuver brought the cowboys' heads together with another solid thud. When Vickery released them, their knees gave way, and they dropped to the floor like bags of potatoes. The captain stood above the unconscious trio shaking his head.

"Somebody ought to take these boys outside and cool 'em off in a waterin' trough. I'd be glad to do it, but a man of my age might strain his back or somethin'."

He reseated himself at the table when the bartender vaulted the bar and hurried toward the cowhands.

"What are you gawkin' at, son?" Vickery's growl was directed at the waiter who stood staring with his jaw sagging. "I think my friend and me ordered us a couple of steaks. We'd like to have 'em for dinner, not breakfast. And shut your mouth. You're liable to catch yourself a couple of flies if'n you don't."

Cody's hand lifted from his still-holstered Colt. He made no attempt to disguise the admiration in his voice when he said, "Cap'n, remind me never to get on your bad side. Or offer to buy you a beer ever again."

Vickery winked at his colleague. "Cody, as you well know, I've been known to enjoy a brew or two and even a snort of corn squeezin's now 'n then. I just don't believe in a man forcin' himself on another." The captain watched the bartender drag the last of the three cowboys into the street. "This world would be a mite more peaceable if folks were left alone to live like they saw fit. The trouble is there's always someone only too willin' to try and make a man do somethin' he don't want to do."

Cody nodded. "I reckon that's why you and me do what we do."

•   •   •

The hotel room was small, but clean. It was also new enough to still smell of pine. After buying a bath at a barbershop a few stores away from the hotel, Cody returned to the Three Rivers and climbed the stairs to his second-floor room, undressed, then stretched out on the soft luxury of a feather bed.

Accustomed to working alone—a lone wolf, he'd heard Vickery call him—Cody found himself plagued by doubts about his present assignment. To begin with, it wasn't so much an assignment as it was an accident. Had any other member of Company C been in Del Rio to receive the telegram from Eldorado, that Ranger would be in San Angelo rather than Cody.

Of course, the murderous butcher who seemed determined to single-handedly spread a trail of blood across Texas had to be stopped. But Cody felt uncomfortable. Working with a partner in a case and having to confer on matters instead of choosing his own course to take was hard enough. Now he was also a subordinate who couldn't act unless it was on the orders of his superior.

During dinner the two Rangers had discussed how they intended to approach locating the killer in San Angelo—if the killer indeed was here in town. Until the towns between San Angelo and El Paso were checked, they couldn't be certain of the killer's location. He, or she, could be in El Paso or on another stagecoach headed west by now. About the only conclusion they did reach was that for the time being they'd keep their Ranger identities hidden.

Still troubled by the worries that ate at his mind, Cody at last got rest when sleep overcame him.

Captain Vickery sat in a chair beside his open window and stared down at the street below. Though his eyes saw the soldiers and cowboys wandering from saloon to saloon, his mind was elsewhere.

He didn't like to admit it even to himself, but he was

frightened. Not a shaking-in-his-boots fear. What he feared was failure.

The killer he sought wasn't some fast gun or cattle rustler or Comanche raider. Those he understood and could handle. He knew what made hardcases of their ilk tick. He remembered his excitement when he'd ridden from Del Rio, thinking this assignment would be no different from trailing any other desperado he'd ever gone after and eventually ridden down. He glanced down at his bare chest. His encounter with the killer in that Eldorado alley had taught him how different the maniac he sought was.

Vickery stood and crossed to the bed. Stretching out, he closed his eyes and began making a mental list of things Cody and he needed to do tomorrow. Towns along the stage line should be wired to see if the killer had struck west of San Angelo. If so, he and Cody were wasting their time where they were. If not, the Rangers would introduce themselves to the local sheriff. It wouldn't hurt to have a few extra eyes to keep tabs on the passengers he'd met on the stage.

Vickery didn't see a need to remain undercover any longer. Sometimes a Ranger badge had a way of making a wanted man nervous. Nervous men made mistakes. And, Vickery feared, a few mistakes might be needed to get a handle on this killer. The trouble was that those mistakes might not come until the butcher killed again.

CHAPTER 7

Cody was a light sleeper. Whether it was by nature or by self-preserving instinct as a Ranger hardly mattered. What did matter was that it had saved his life on more than one occasion. When the door to his room opened sometime in the middle of the night, he immediately responded, reaching behind his head to the bedpost and the holstered Colt hanging there. But before he could grab the pistol, a hand slammed into his arm, knocking the weapon away.

"Don't you even think about it, friend," ordered a voice he had never heard before. "That is, if you want to live to see mornin'."

The familiar metallic click of a cocking pistol sounded an instant before a cold, hard gun barrel was pressed firmly to his left temple.

"I got no reason to be usin' this at the moment," the voice said. "Don't go and give me one. Neither one of us'd like the consequences."

The light spilling in from the hallway revealed two men, one on each side of the bed. And though the backlighting didn't provide much detail, Cody could see enough to determine that both men had revolvers drawn, and the expression of the one holding a gun to his head indicated that he wouldn't hesitate using the weapon if provoked. Unarmed and naked except for his drawers, Cody had no wish to rile the man—or even provide him with the thought that he *might* be riled.

"What is this?" Cody asked, finally finding his voice. "What's going on?"

The man to Cody's left lifted the Ranger's Colt from the holster and tossed it across the room. "That's what the sheriff will be wantin' to ask you down at the jail. So get out of that bed and get dressed."

"The sheriff?" Cody looked from one to the other, noticing the badges on their chests for the first time. "Why would the sheriff want to question me?"

"You'll find out soon enough when we get you to the jail," said the man to his right. "Now, get yourself up and into your pants. We ain't got all night to be waitin' on you."

Doing as ordered, Cody cautiously climbed from the bed, making certain he made no quick moves that might be misinterpreted as a sudden break. With slow deliberation, he took his blue work shirt that was draped on the chair and slipped it on, then pulled on his jeans, his socks, and his boots.

He considered telling the two he was a Texas Ranger, then pushed the thought away. Captain Vickery had yet to decide whether or not they were working undercover. Until Cody knew what the situation was, it was best to keep his mouth shut.

"Come on, get a move on," one of the deputies said, prodding him to his feet with a pistol muzzle. "Soon as you're locked away, we'll be back for your partner."

Cody was only mildly surprised to hear them speak of Vickery. Of course they would know about the captain, he thought. They'd obviously been keeping an eye out for any strangers in town—thanks to the warning telegram that they themselves had suggested Sheriff MacArt send to the San Angelo sheriff.

The irony of the situation was not lost on Cody as he was roughly hustled off to jail.

"Friend, you're making a mighty big mistake," Captain Vickery growled as the two deputies pushed him into a cell already packed with ten men. "This is no way to treat a fellow officer of the law."

"Old man, if you're a Texas Ranger," a deputy said as he locked the cell, "then I'm Sam-by-God-Houston himself!"

Cody, standing in an equally packed cell opposite the one holding Vickery, was about to toss off a caustic reply, something to the effect that Sam Houston might not appreciate being compared with a feeble-brained deputy, but thought better of it. Still, with Vickery having tried to convince the overzealous deputies of his identity, he saw no reason to remain silent. He stepped to the bars and said to the deputy, "He's more than just a Ranger. That man's Cap'n Wallace Vickery, commander of Company C of the Texas Ranger Frontier Battalion out of Del Rio."

"And I suppose you're a Ranger, too?" Sarcasm lay thick in the deputy's words.

"Ranger Sam Cody," Cody said. "Cap'n Vickery and me're here on orders from Major John Jones in San Antonio, who commands all of the Frontier Battalion."

"You got to admit them two have some imaginations," the deputy hooted. "Never arrested no one claimin' to be a Ranger before—and now I got myself two in the same night." He paused and looked at the four crowded cells. "Any others of you drifters and no-accounts think you're Texas Rangers?"

The deputy received a chorus of curses in reply, provoking a snicker from the second deputy.

"Forget it, Cody. They won't listen to words," Vickery growled from his cell. "The worthless alley dogs wouldn't even let me open my valise and show 'em my badge."

Cody reached into a pocket and withdrew his watch. "Would a badge convince you two that we're telling our story straight?"

He opened the watch, unscrewed the picture in its cover, and removed the silver star hidden within. He pinned it to his shirt. "Ranger Sam Cody, like I said before. Now, would you let Cap'n Vickery and me out of here?"

"A fancy badge don't make a man a Texas Ranger," said a gruff voice from the entry to the cellblock. Cody turned toward the doorway to the jail and saw a middle-aged man with a thick head of black hair, silvered at the temples, standing there. "Anyone could get a silversmith to carve him up a badge so he could go around play-actin' at bein' a lawman. A badge might get a few doors open for a slick operator." The man entered the cellblock and studied Cody. "It'll take more than a tin star to get me to open that cell." Turning to stare at Vickery, he added, "A badge in some valise holds no more weight."

The newcomer, himself wearing a star pinned to a brown leather vest, walked up and down the cells, scrutinizing those crammed within. "I don't recognize a one of your faces, which is why you're here."

The man paused and stood beside the deputies. "I'm Earl Lee Whittington, and I'm sheriff of San Angelo. Have been for nigh on a year now, and I'd like to keep this job for a while. The only trouble is, one of you worthless whoresons has gone and made it uncomfortable for me. If I don't put an end to what you've been up to, folks around these parts'll start thinkin' that maybe it's time ol' Earl Lee found himself another job."

Cody thought that something didn't ring true in the sheriff's voice. Underneath the casual bravado was a note of uncertainty.

"Every one of you brought in tonight—or this mornin' as the case may be—is a stranger in San Angelo. That means you got no one to vouch for you," the sheriff continued. "In my book that also means one of you is the bloodiest murderin' bastard that ever rode into this town. It also means there ain't a one of you goin' to walk in the light of day until I learn which one of you has been butcherin' the good citizens of San Angelo. Every last one of you sons of bitches can stay in those cells and rot for all I care. And that's what you'll do until I have my killer. So if any one of you knows somethin' about the bastard I want, speak up."

Vickery took advantage of Whittington's pause to say, "A couple of days back you received a telegram from Sheriff Sean MacArt down in Eldorado. He warned you this might happen."

"Sean did say somethin' about—" Sheriff Whittington stopped abruptly and spun around to face the captain. "How'd you know about that wire, friend?"

"Because I was the one who suggested Sheriff MacArt send that wire. It warned you that the Johnson Line stage was bringin' trouble your way. The name's Captain Wallace Vickery."

Cody saw Whittington's face falter for an instant with uncertainty. Then the lawman shook his head. "If you and your friend there are Rangers, then you'll have to accept my apologies. But knowin' about Sean's message ain't enough to get you out of that cell. Anyone could've found out about the wire."

Vickery grabbed the cell's bars with both hands, his face reddening angrily, but Cody spoke up before the captain exploded in rage. "Major Jones in San Antonio can vouch for us. He assigned Company C the job of bringing in your killer, Sheriff. If you'd wire him, he'd put things straight."

Whittington rubbed at his chin. He finally nodded. "I'll give you the benefit of the doubt. Come mornin', I'll wire San Antonio. But until I get an answer, you two have yourselves a home behind these bars."

He turned and walked toward the doorway, saying to the deputies, "Welch, start bringin' these lowlifes to my office one at a time, startin' with the one claimin' to be a Ranger captain. We'll listen to what each one has to say for himself, even if it takes the rest of the night and the whole of the day. And Todman, at first light I want you to ride out to the Kingston place and tell Lisa that her daddy's been murdered. Break it to her as gently as you can. This ain't goin' to be easy for her, what with her mama dyin' less than a year back."

Whittington and Deputy Todman left the cellblock, and Deputy Welch, pistol drawn again, opened the cell holding Vickery. He motioned the Ranger outside. "Guess you heard the sheriff, old man. He wants to start with you."

Standing stiffly erect, Vickery sauntered out of his cell. He caught Cody's eye and told him, "I'll have you out of there in no time, son. Don't you worry none."

"I have every confidence in you, Cap'n," Cody replied and watched Vickery walk toward Whittington's office, escorted by the gun-toting deputy.

Finding an unused piece of wall, Cody leaned against it. He took out his pocket watch and opened it. Three A.M. He sighed. It was going to be a long night and an equally long morning. Truth was, he wasn't all that sure that Vickery would convince Whittington of their identities, since that hinged on Major Jones's confirmation. What if Jones wasn't in San Antonio? What if he was up in Austin to speak before the state legislature, as he often was? Or on his way to somewhere else, making him incommunicado for who knew how long?

Cody closed his eyes and tried to push those scenarios from his mind. If Jones *was* unavailable, he didn't want to consider how long he might be locked up in a crowded cell with a bunch of unsavory characters who didn't exactly admire lawmen. . . .

Fingers nudged Cody's right shoulder, jarring him from sleep. The Ranger, who sat on the floor of the cell with his back against the wall, glanced over. Deputy Welch squatted outside the cell, his hand dangling inside the bars.

"Sheriff Whittington wants you in his office," the deputy said as he stood. "He got that answer from San Antonio . . . Ranger."

Cody's stiff back protested when he rose from the floor, but that didn't erase the smile of relief from his face. While Welch opened the door to Cody's cell, Deputy Todman opened the door to Vickery's. The older Ranger was scowling, but Cody saw the same relief that he felt mirrored in the captain's eyes.

The two Rangers were escorted through the cellblock into the sheriff's office, where Whittington stood beside his desk with a yellow telegram flimsy in his right hand and chagrin on his face. Cody glanced at the Regulator clock on the wall above the sheriff's desk. It was eleven-thirty. That meant nine hours, almost to the minute, had passed since they'd first been locked up.

"Seems as how I was a bit hasty lockin' you fellas up last night." All the hardness that had been evident in Whittington's voice during his earlier, hour-long interro-

gation of Cody and Vickery was suddenly gone. "Seein'
as how you two already know what the two murders I've
got on my hands are like, I reckon you can understand why
I did what I did last night."

That was as close to an apology as the sheriff was going
to make for having jailed two fellow lawmen, Cody realized. Whittington had made a mistake, but he wasn't going
to admit it. A glance at Vickery's expression said that the
captain didn't expect more from the sheriff either.

"Sheriff, what I don't understand is why you weren't
ready for what happened," Vickery said. "MacArt sent that
telegram warnin' you a killer was comin' your way."

Whittington nodded. "And I took that wire seriously. I
was waitin' at the stage office when the stagecoach rolled
into town. I knew everyone who got off the coach except
for a new schoolmarm, some tinhorn gambler, and a Negro
Army lieutenant assigned to Fort Concho. Now, understand,
Captain, that there's only me and my two deputies here. A
town like San Angelo needs four times that many men to
hold a tight rein on it. We've done our best to keep an eye
on them three, but we can't watch 'em day and night and
tend to our other duties besides."

Cody mentally shook his head. Whittington understood
the horror this killer had left in his wake, but he hadn't
grasped what he was up against. The killer was a madman—
or madwoman—which meant that any one of those leaving
the stage here in San Angelo could be the killer, not just
the three newcomers to town.

"What are you goin' do with those men in there?" Vickery
asked, looking over a shoulder to the doorway leading to
the cells.

"Keep 'em right where they are," Whittington replied.
"It occurred to me that the man I'm lookin' for could be
someone followin' the stage."

Vickery nodded. "The same thought had passed my
mind."

Whittington cleared his throat as he sat on the edge of
his desk. "I know you two men have been workin' on
these murders, but they're happenin' in San Angelo now,
and that makes 'em my business. I was hopin' we might

be able to work together and bring this bastard in to be hanged."

"Cody and I never had any intention of doin' other than workin' with you, Sheriff," Vickery said.

Actually, Cody thought, turning his head to look at the captain, that was the first time Vickery had mentioned anything at all about how they'd handle the case.

Whittington sounded relieved. "I'm much obliged, Captain. I reckon you'd like to sit in on a meetin' I've set up with some officers from Fort Concho to see what they can do to help out."

"The Army?" Vickery's eyes narrowed. "You've brought the Army in on this?"

Whittington shrugged. "Didn't have a choice. It was the Army that found the man who was killed last night. A local rancher named Calvin Kingston."

From the captain's expression Cody could tell Vickery didn't like Army involvement any more than he himself did. Soldiers weren't trained as law officers.

"When is this meetin'?" Vickery asked.

The sheriff glanced up at the clock. "About an hour from now—here."

Vickery glanced at his colleague. "That'll give me and Cody time to get back to the hotel and get some lunch . . . especially seein' as how we missed breakfast," he added meaningfully. "We'll be here in time for your meetin'."

"The facts as we know 'em are this," Sheriff Whittington said as he outlined the events that led to the rancher's murder. "It was Calvin Kingston's poker night. He and a few friends got together for a neighborly game each week—as much an excuse for friends to get together, chew the fat, and share a few drinks as play cards, since the stakes were nothin' to speak of. The game broke up around midnight, and Calvin mounted his old roan and started back to his ranch like he always did. None of the others at the game noticed nothin' unusual. They didn't see nobody followin' him."

"Maybe it was one of the others in the game who followed

him?" U.S. Army Major Wendell Dutton suggested, receiving a nod of approval from Captain Thomas Harrington, seated at his side.

"Already thought of that," Whittington said with a shake of his head. "All six men who played cards with Calvin have wives to vouch for the time they returned home. All of 'em were in bed by twelve-fifteen."

"When was Kingston's body found?" Captain Vickery asked.

"At approximately one in the morning," Major Dutton answered. "He was found by a young lieutenant recently arrived at the fort, a Lieutenant Harper. The lieutenant and a small company of men were on a routine night patrol. They had bivouacked about five miles south of town near the river. The lieutenant had been unable to sleep and went for a walk. It was then that he discovered Mr. Kingston's body, close by the river. He immediately returned to camp and sent a rider to the fort to apprise his superiors of the situation. In turn, you were informed, Sheriff Whittington."

While the men in the room discussed the grisly details of Kingston's murder—details that matched the other killings that had occurred, including missing ears—Cody looked over at the sole female in the office. Lisa Kingston, sitting quietly on the other side of the room, was the type of woman who would have drawn the Ranger's attention even if the room had been filled with females.

Though her green eyes were rimmed with red from crying, no tears rolled down her fair cheeks now as she sat straight in a chair, following every word uttered. She was one of those women whose inner distinction—a remarkable strength—was more immediately evident than was any outward distinction.

Which was not to say that Lisa Kingston was an unattractive woman, Cody thought; it was just that her beauty didn't strike a man at first glance. But by the third glance any man not seeing that beauty would have to be blind. Striking was the word that came to mind as Cody studied the young woman's high cheekbones, strong nose, and generous mouth. Her hair, which hung loose about her shoulders, was auburn with threads of gold running through it. She wore a white blouse tucked into faded blue denims, and though no doubt some would have found fault with her attire, Cody thought that, if anything, the denims and blouse revealed more of her feminine form than a dress and petticoats ever would have.

"Gentlemen," Lisa put in, "I understand the need to go over details, but I don't see where you're headed. You've established that my father was riding home from his weekly poker game. You've determined he was killed sometime around twelve-thirty this morning. And you know an Army officer found his body. But there hasn't been a single mention of anything that might lead to the man who killed him. What about a trail? Footprints? Hoof prints?"

The men fell silent. Embarrassed glances shot between them.

Whittington eventually cleared his throat and said, "Miss Lisa, we found nothin' except your father. Whoever killed him made certain he didn't leave so much as a single track. I found a cut stalk of broomweed on the riverbank nearby. I suspect the man that did this used it to brush away what few tracks he'd have left. I say 'what few tracks' 'cause I believe the killer followed Calvin from town, either on foot or horseback, and traveled for the most part in the Concho River's shallows near the bank. My guess is that he used the broomweed to sweep away any tracks he left immediately by the body as he retreated back into the river, then came back to town the same way he left. Me and my deputies rode along the river for miles in both directions but couldn't find a trail. The killer probably entered and left the river at a well-used crossing."

Lisa turned to Vickery and Cody. "And what do you Rangers make of the situation? Did you find anything more than the sheriff?"

Vickery spoke before Cody could open his mouth. "I'm sorry, ma'am. Neither me nor Ranger Cody has ridden out to where your father was killed. Both of us were, uh, detained until about an hour ago."

For several seconds Lisa sat silently staring at her hands, which rested on her knees. When she looked up, she said,

"Gentlemen, I'm sure that the Army, Sheriff Whittington, and the Texas Rangers will do everything possible to catch my father's killer. But tomorrow morning at my father's funeral his casket will have its lid closed so that none of his friends can see what some mad butcher did to him. I want every one of you to know that if you can't bring in the person who did this, I'll hire someone who can do the job—even if it takes every cent I've got."

With that she stood and walked to the door. Turning, she looked back at the men who hurriedly stood from their chairs. "I'm not trying to cut any of you down," she told them. "I just want to see that my father's killer gets what he deserves. Good day, gentlemen."

Captain Harrington whistled softly when the door closed behind Lisa. "I do believe that young lady meant what she said."

"She did," Whittington answered. "Calvin Kingston was a headstrong man who went after something until he got it. He didn't have himself but one child—and he raised her up to be the same way."

CHAPTER
8

Deputy Todman entered the sheriff's office with a piece of paper in his hand. He crossed the room, unfolded the paper, and placed it on the sheriff's desk. Without looking up, Whittington spread it smooth beside another piece of paper already on the desk. For a few moments his eyes shifted between the columns of names written on the two pieces of paper.

Clearing his throat, Whittington looked up and told Vickery, "Your list checks out with the stage line's passenger list."

Cody saw Vickery's neck turn red. Had Whittington been a Ranger in his command, Vickery would've chewed the man out for questioning his superior's memory. As it was, the captain's words came out in a controlled growl. "I ain't quite gone senile, Sheriff. I can remember who was on that stage with me."

"I didn't expect you wouldn't," Whittington replied, equally gruffly. "Just wanted to double-check the names is all. Could be someone was pullin' a fast one and usin' another name."

Whittington opened a desk drawer and took a "two-fer" from a wooden box. Putting the cheap cigar between his teeth, he chewed at it rather than lighting the smoke. He glanced back at the two lists and shook his head. "Like I said earlier, I can vouch for everybody who got off the stage except this new Army lieutenant, the gambler, and the schoolteacher. Known all of them since I came to San

Angelo two years ago. Got to know 'em even better in the year I've been sheriffin'. They're good people."

The red on Vickery's neck darkened. "Sheriff, in case you weren't listenin' before when I said this, I'm goin' to say it again: Whoever's doin' these killings ain't no sane man or woman, though I reckon they act just as sane as you or me most of the time—till they get a knife in their hand. We can't cross anybody off those lists, not until we have the killer locked in your jail, waitin' for the hangman."

Whittington glanced at the door leading to the cells. "Could be we already got our killer locked up. If he was someone followin' the stage for some reason—maybe to get at one of the passengers."

The more Cody heard the stranger-riding-after-the-stage theory, the more it sounded like a bucket with a thousand or two holes in its bottom. Why would someone following the stage butcher the people that he had if all he wanted to do was kill one of the stage's passengers? It simply didn't add up.

"I ain't discardin' that idea, but I think we got a stronger case pointin' at one of those seven people," Vickery said, pointing to the lists. "I think we should start by havin' ourselves a talk with each of those folks and see where they were the nights that the cowboy and the rancher were killed."

Vickery had sent telegrams out to sheriffs between San Angelo and El Paso to see if similar murders had occurred farther down the line. To Cody those wires were merely a routine check to confirm something he already knew: The murderer was now in San Angelo and would continue his bloody work until he was stopped.

Whittington stroked his neck as though considering possibilities. "Reckon you're right," he finally said. "We've got to cover all angles on this. If we don't catch ourselves a killer soon, the good people of San Angelo'll be wantin' to hang *us*."

Cody glanced away to hide his disdainful expression. It wasn't Vickery's or Cody's neck the sheriff was worried about, it was his own.

"Why don't the three of us divide up these names and go

and do some talkin'?" Whittington finally suggested to the Rangers. He looked at his deputies, telling them, "You two try and keep a lid on the town while we're gone." Turning back to Vickery, he added, "I'm still not sure this is goin' to do any good. I know most of these people. If the killer was a passenger on that stage, then I'll place my money on the gambler or that uppity buffalo soldier."

Captain Harrington pushed from his desk and stood as Cody entered his office at Fort Concho. The Army officer didn't hide his concern about the fort being invaded by a civil law officer.

"I suspected one of you Rangers would be paying us a visit sooner or later. I guess there's no way to keep the Army out of this, is there?"

Cody shook his head. " 'Fraid not. I have to question Lieutenant Harper just like the other stage passengers have to be questioned."

"Harper's a West Point man, you know," Harrington said. "For some people that means more than the color of his skin. He's a commissioned officer in the United States Army and deserves the respect that comes with that rank."

"I only want to ask him a few questions. I'm not dressed in white sheets and a white hood." Cody could well imagine what a Negro West Point graduate meant to some lily-white Army officers—especially those assigned to Fort Concho with its buffalo soldiers. A burr under a saddle couldn't have rubbed them more raw. "I'm only doing my job. The same job I'd be doing if *you'd* been on that stage."

Harrington stiffened for a moment, then called for a sergeant, who came to the door. "Sergeant Duval will escort you to Lieutenant Harper's quarters. And, Ranger, don't keep my officer too long. He has duties to attend to just like every other man in this fort."

Cody nodded and followed the black sergeant outside into the late-afternoon sunlight. Fort Concho looked no different from any other fort in Texas the Ranger had ever visited. There were barracks for the enlisted men, individual houses for married officers, houses shared by unmarried officers, a sutler's store, stables, parade grounds, and storage buildings.

"Lieutenant Harper's bivouacked over yonder in that tent behind the bachelor officers' quarters," the sergeant at Cody's side said in an accent out of the deep South, pointing toward the tent. "Officially, he's waitin' for one of them rooms inside to free up," the sergeant added, his tone somewhat acerbic.

Harper would probably still be waiting for that room when his hair had turned gray, Cody thought. Apparently the color of a man's skin mattered more than his rank when it came to sleeping quarters at Fort Concho.

"A Texas Ranger!" the sergeant suddenly said with a doleful shake of his head. "I knew no good'd come of bringin' a black officer out here. He's been here less than a week, and the Army's already got the law on his tail."

Cody eyed the soldier. "I'm only here to talk with the lieutenant."

"That's what I heard you say," the sergeant replied sardonically.

They reached Harper's tent, and the sergeant stepped to the closed flap to announce the officer's visitor.

A deep voice responded, "Ranger Cody, you may enter."

Cody lifted the tent flap and stepped inside. "Cody will do. 'Ranger' isn't a rank."

"Cody, then." Harper, who stood beside a small field desk at the back of the tent, gave a crisp nod. "Captain Harrington suggested earlier that someone might be by today to question me."

The Ranger couldn't place Harper's accent, but it was definitely northern, educated, and brimming with arrogance. He expected the latter; arrogance seemed to plague all young Army officers until the Texas sun had a chance to dry the wet behind their ears. That was, if they lived that long. Though from Harper's appearance, he'd have a better chance than most. Tall and muscular, clean-shaven and with closely trimmed hair, he gave off an air of being completely in command of a situation. Despite his dusty surroundings, even his uniform was immaculate, each brass button polished and gleaming.

"You may sit if you wish," Harper suggested, settling into the only chair within the tent.

That left Cody having to perch himself on the edge of the lieutenant's cot—which he did without hesitating. If Harper's gesture was an attempt at an insult or domination, Cody ignored it. "Captain Harrington said I wasn't to take up too much of your time, so I'll get right to the point. Tell me about last night."

"There isn't anything to add to what I already reported," Harper replied. He sat stiffly in his chair. "My command was on routine patrol of the area, and we had camped for the night. It was stiflingly hot. After trying unsuccessfully to sleep for an hour, I gave up and decided to go for a walk. About a mile or so from the camp, I found the rancher's body. I returned to camp and ordered a rider to the fort to inform my superiors of my discovery."

"You took your walk alone?" Cody asked.

"As I'm sure you're aware, this is no longer a hostile area. I saw no reason for a personal guard."

"You would have if you'd stepped on a rattler." Cody's comment was a small pin meant to deflate the lieutenant's ego.

It missed its mark. Harper sat even more rigid in the chair. "There was no rattlesnake. Just a naked man who had been butchered like some animal."

"Did you notice anything in the area around Kingston's body?"

"Nothing at all. In fact, it appeared to have been swept clean."

"What about two nights before that?" Cody asked. "Where were you then?"

"I was here in the fort. Why?"

"A cowhand was killed that night. Cut up the same as Kingston."

Harper's eyes widened. "The rancher wasn't an isolated incident? I didn't realize there had been another murder."

"There've been five others besides the cowboy," Cody said. "Killed along the route taken by the stage you rode to San Angelo."

The lieutenant's eyes abruptly narrowed as the Ranger's

meaning hit home. "And you believe I am responsible for those murders?"

Cody shrugged. "I believe *someone* on that stage is. You happened to be on the stage. Can you account for your time during the stopovers in these towns?"

As the Ranger listed the towns where the killer's knife had struck, he watched tiny beads of sweat pop up on Harper's brow. The young officer's arrogance began to dissolve.

The lieutenant's gaze searched out different corners of the tent as though he were trying to search out hidden corners of his memory. "I'm not certain of details," he said. "I usually had my meals at the way stations—that is, behind the way stations. I often took walks. My legs cramped from sitting atop the stagecoach, you see. I needed to stretch and work out the kinks."

"Were other passengers with you?"

Harper laughed humorlessly. "Ranger, I'm a black-skinned man, in case you haven't noticed. Because of that I couldn't ride with the other passengers or even take my meals with them. So what do you think? Most of the others on the stage didn't even give me the time of day. Texas hospitality doesn't extend to a Negro, Ranger—especially one wearing the uniform of an officer in the United States Army. I've risen above what you Texans see as my station in life. I don't say 'yes, massah' to any man."

Cody wasn't certain how to respond. He didn't deny the hate and mistrust of blacks in the state, even in regions where buffalo soldiers had guarded the frontier against Indian attack. The years of carpetbaggers after the war had done nothing to heal open wounds; they only sprinkled salt into them.

"You can check with the other passengers regarding my activities during the journey here, but I doubt they'll speak for me," Harper concluded. "As far as my actions in San Angelo, there are officers and soldiers who will vouch for me. Check with them. Now, if there's nothing else, I have my duties. After all, that's why the United States Army trained me."

Cody nodded. It was clear he'd get nothing else from

the officer by pressing him. "That's enough for now," he agreed. "But unless someone walks into the jail and gives himself up, I suspect we'll be talking again."

Rising from the cot, he walked outside to where the sergeant still waited. Speaking loudly enough for Harper to overhear, the Ranger said, "Sergeant, I'd like to see Captain Harrington again. I need to speak with a few of the men who've been serving with Lieutenant Harper."

The young officer inside the tent was already sweating, Cody thought. No harm in letting him sweat a little more. After all, Harper had been close to a murder scene—a fact that didn't brand him the killer, but didn't eliminate him, either. Though it seemed unlikely that if Harper were the murderer he'd have called attention to the body he had apparently accidentally stumbled on, maybe that was the whole idea. Maybe it was a clever, calculated plan by a clever, calculating man.

Cody went next to the enlisted men's barracks, hoping to check out Harper's account and make certain that the young officer hadn't failed to mention something he'd rather leave unsaid. Most of the troopers who'd been on patrol with Harper that night were available, and it didn't take long for Cody to question them and determine that Harper's account matched those of his men.

With no further avenues to explore at the moment regarding his first suspect, Cody mounted up and headed back to town—though his second suspect seemed even less likely a candidate as a murderer: the Reverend Jacob Mason, a well-respected, long-standing citizen of San Angelo.

Cody had no trouble finding the Mason home, thanks to directions given him previously by the sheriff. He tied his horse to a hitching post out front, then climbed the steps to the wraparound porch of the two-story house. As he stood by the front door, Cody caught a sweet floral scent wafting in the air. He sniffed deeply several times, trying to identify it, and finally recognized it as jasmine, a scent his mother often used. The scent became stronger when a plain-looking middle-aged woman answered his knock and opened the door.

"May I help you?" she asked, an uncertain smile on her

face as she looked from his face to the star pinned on his vest and back again.

"Sorry to disturb you, ma'am. Are you Mrs. Mason?"

"Yes, I'm Clara Mason, and you aren't disturbing me at all, Ranger," she assured him politely. "I do hope nothing is wrong."

"Oh, no, ma'am. My name's Cody, and I'd just like to speak with your husband. I won't take up much of his time."

"Certainly. Follow me."

Cody removed his hat as the Reverend Jacob Mason's wife led him inside to a small, cluttered parlor, where the smell of jasmine was overpowering. The scent came not only from the perfume Clara Mason wore, but from sticks of incense burning in a container atop one of the parlor tables.

"It's the West Texas dust," Clara explained, noticing Cody eyeing the incense. "It gets inside a house no matter what a body does, and the smell is so repugnant to me. So I burn incense to cover it." She smiled. "My husband teases me that burning incense is a sign that I still have a touch of the heathen in me."

"And your husband is . . . ?"

"Jacob is upstairs in his study, working on next Sunday's sermon. I'll get him for you. Please make yourself comfortable." The small woman, dressed in a gray dress so dark that it was almost black, hurried from the room. The click of her low heels echoed through the house as she climbed the runnerless wooden steps.

Moments later heavier footfalls announced Jacob Mason's arrival. Cody stood as a stern-faced, thin, wiry man dressed in black pants, black vest, and white shirt entered the room.

Cody introduced himself again and explained, "Reverend, I have a few questions to ask you about your trip back from Arkansas."

The preacher turned to his brown-haired wife. "Clara, it's such a warm day. Do you think we might have a glass of lemonade?"

"Of course, Jacob." She scurried toward the kitchen as Mason waved Cody to an overstuffed chair.

"What type of questions do you have concerning my journey, Mr. Cody?"

Cody quickly described the series of murders that had occurred and his suspicion that the murderer had traveled on the stage to San Angelo.

The minister arched an eyebrow. "I see. And because I was returning from my older sister's funeral on that stage, I am a suspected murderer?"

"I'm afraid that's the size of it, Reverend," Cody replied. If he had expected outrage, it wasn't evident either in Mason's voice or expression. "I need to know your whereabouts in each of those towns where a killing took place and if any of the other passengers can verify your actions."

Pursing his lips, Mason sank back in his chair and tented his fingers. "This is a somewhat awkward position for a man of the cloth to find himself in, Mr. Cody. My congregation would not look favorably on their parson being suspected of brutal slayings."

"There's not much I can do about that," Cody said. "But if you could recount how you spent your time in those towns, I'm certain it'll help put things straight."

Mason momentarily closed his dark eyes and finally gave a firm nod. "You're right, of course. I'll cooperate in any way that I can. Let me think a minute. I can't recall doing anything out of the ordinary. For the most part the stage ride was long and jostling."

"And *in* the towns?" Cody asked, guiding the minister back to the point.

Mason shrugged. "Nothing out of the ordinary that I can remember. I took my meals in the way stations and went for an occasional walk. For the most part the passengers went their own way." The minister gave a small smile, adding, "I suspect we tired of looking at one another day after day."

Cody sighed. Mason's recollections were practically the same as Harper's, minus the young lieutenant's bitterness.

"Wait!" Mason suddenly exclaimed, sitting straight in the chair. "The night in Texarkana, several of us attended a sermon in a tent. I don't remember the others, but I do recall Miss Wakefield, our new schoolteacher, being there. I think Harry Farris, one of San Angelo's merchants, was there as well, as were two ranchers from New Mexico. It was a Sunday evening, and the circuit preacher's tent was the only house of God available. In fact, after I introduced myself to—" Mason paused a moment as though lost in thought, then shook his head. "I'm afraid I can't recall the preacher's name, but he asked me to deliver a short opening message. I believe I spoke of the Sermon on the Mount and the bounty to be found in the Lord Jesus."

Cody made a mental note to check with Miss Wakefield and Farris about the sermon. "I suppose you've heard about the murders here in San Angelo?" he asked. "Two men killed in the same manner as the others."

Surprise washed across the preacher's face. "Two more murders took place here in town?"

"One last night and one two nights ago," Cody said. "The first was a cowhand from a nearby ranch. Last night a rancher named Calvin Kingston was found a few miles from town."

"Calvin Kingston!" Mason gasped. "Calvin and his family were members of my congregation. His wife died suddenly less than a year ago. Oh, dear! What their poor daughter must be going through! I will have to call on Lisa to offer spiritual comfort and see what funeral arrangements have been made."

Cody was surprised that Miss Kingston hadn't already visited her family's parson. On the other hand, the young woman had spent a large part of the afternoon in the sheriff's office trying to find out what was being done to capture her father's killer.

"I'm sure she will appreciate your concern, Reverend," the Ranger said, eyeing the preacher. "And I'm sorry to have to ask you this, but where were you last night and two nights ago, when these men were killed?"

"He was at home, Mr. Cody," Clara Mason answered for her husband as she entered the parlor, holding a tray with two glasses of lemonade. She handed one glass to the Ranger and the other to the preacher. "Where else would Jacob be? He was here in his home with me."

Mason glanced at Cody and nodded. "My wife is correct, Mr. Cody. Except for occasional church duties, neither one of us goes out at night very much. San Angelo's streets aren't safe for God-fearing people after the sun goes down."

The Ranger took a sip of the lemonade. He could barely taste it over the cloying scent of jasmine that filled the house. He quickly drained the glass and stood, saying, "Well, that should be it for now. I thank you for your time. And for the lemonade, Mrs. Mason." He handed the glass to Clara, then turned to the preacher. "It might be necessary to talk with you again to help us find the man doing these killings."

"Anytime, Mr. Cody," Mason said as he stood as well. He shook the Ranger's hand.

"Also, if you remember anything unusual about your trip, let me know," Cody added. "You can find me down at the sheriff's office."

He left the house and breathed deeply. Even smelling of dust, the air outside was a lot easier to breathe than the almost choking jasmine-scented atmosphere in the Mason house. Shaking his head in amazement at what some people considered a normal way of living, the tall Ranger strode down the front walk. Untying his mount, he headed for the sheriff's office.

Inside the Three Rivers One's saloon Cody sipped at a warm beer that had long ago lost its head, listening to Captain Vickery and Sheriff Whittington report on their questioning of the other stagecoach passengers. Like Cody, they had come up empty-handed. It seemed as though all the passengers could account for their time while traveling to San Angelo, but not one of them could corroborate any of the others' stories.

"I don't know what I expected," Vickery said. "A man doesn't go lookin' for an alibi for himself unless he knows he's goin' to need one." He took a sip of his own beer. "There was no reason for them to keep an eye on one another while they were on the stage."

"Damn!" Whittington spat, shoving away a half-finished beer. "I would've sworn that tinhorn gambler was the one.

But the son of a bitch has at least five men who put him at a poker table the nights of the two killin's here."

"It seems that the killer deliberately timed his absences so he'd go unnoticed," Cody suggested. "And he works fast. In Eldorado he killed one woman—and was about to do the same to the captain here—and mutilated her in what couldn't have been more than fifteen minutes. And then he managed to clean himself up and was on the stage when it pulled out."

Whittington put his glass down with a thump. "It *can't* be one of the passengers. It has to be one of those drifters I've got over in the jail."

Vickery shook his head. "I can't say as I agree with that. Oh, sure, it's possible, but I'd say it's about as slim as a spider's thread."

"So where do we go from here?" Whittington asked, looking back and forth between the two Rangers. "What's our next step?"

"We question the passengers again," Vickery said. "We each switch suspects this time, and then we come back and compare stories detail by detail until we find a hole in one of 'em."

Cody wasn't sure more questioning would uncover anything new, but he said, "At least if we keep ourselves out there so the killer knows we're around, he might not be so ready to pick up his knife again."

Vickery opened his mouth to comment, but the loudly slamming saloon doors stopped him before he could speak and drew his gaze to the entrance. The surprise on his face made Cody turn around to see what he was looking at. It was Lisa Kingston, marching straight toward their table without a glance at the patrons gawking at this woman so brazenly invading a strictly male domain.

"What have you learned?" she demanded when she reached the lawmen. "Have you arrested my father's murderer?"

Whittington stood and pointed toward the door. "Lisa, you don't belong in a place like this. Why don't we step outside where we can talk?"

"We can talk here," she replied, brushing a stray strand

of auburn hair away from her eyes. "A yes or a no will answer my question."

Whittington sighed. "Then it's no."

The young woman's face turned stony. "That's what I thought. My father is lying over at the undertaker's in a closed coffin, and you three are here drinking beer. You call that trying to arrest his killer?"

"Miss Kingston," Cody said, pushing from the table and standing, "we spent the afternoon trying to find something that might lead us to the man who killed your father. Now we're sitting here piecing together what we've learned."

Cody sensed that Lisa barely kept her rage under control as she asked, "And just what is that?"

"The man we're after isn't an ordinary hardcase. He's a cunning monster who makes certain that when he strikes, he leaves virtually nothing behind except a body. Until we have some clues—"

Lisa exploded. "That's what I thought! Not one of you three has the slightest idea who murdered my father! Instead of searching for the killer, you're sitting in this saloon on your backsides because you've got nothing better to do! You're a lamentable bunch!"

"Lisa—" Whittington said, trying to stop her tirade, but the young woman either wasn't listening or didn't care to be stopped.

"San Angelo isn't that big a town. It shouldn't take three trained lawmen all that long to find a killer. I meant what I said this afternoon: If you three can't handle the job, I'll hire someone who can."

"Miss Kingston, it isn't open and spread out like you seem to think," Cody said, trying to reason with her. "We're dealing with a maniac here—a madman. This isn't an ordinary case."

"Texas Rangers aren't supposed to be ordinary men, Mr. Cody," the young woman retorted. "I expect results from men who call themselves Rangers. If you can't solve this case, then let me know. I'll find the man or men who can."

Turning sharply, she strode from the saloon, leaving dozens of open-mouthed stares in her wake.

"That's one spirited young filly," Vickery said with admiration in his voice.

Indeed, Lisa's spirit and determination was what attracted Cody to her, yet he said, "I hope that spirit doesn't get her into something she can't handle. Whoever our killer is, he doesn't seem particular about whether he murders men or women. If she goes and starts stirring things up too much, she's bound to draw attention. I don't think our man would like that—and I'm afraid he might decide to try to make sure she stays quiet."

CHAPTER
9

The killer slipped from behind the church and darted behind a mesquite thicket, squatting on his haunches in the shadows like some dark-coated beast of prey. For hours he had been wrestling against the hunger gnawing inside him that guided his every action.

He fought it no longer.

His eyes firmly fixed on the church, he homed in on a delicately built woman who stepped from the building with two other women. They said their good-byes, and the killer smiled. She would be his this night.

Clara Mason would be his.

He had watched her in church, always listening to the sermons with a look of rapture on her plain face, a dried-up, sexless woman who would allow herself to find pleasure only in her religion. How he hated her, with her devotion. Clara Mason's devout ways were just like his mother's. *His mother!* A mother who ignored the cries of a son brutalized by a stepfather; a mother so religious, a mother so consumed by the words in her well-worn Bible that she viewed sex, even between a husband and wife, as something dirty and unclean; a mother who allowed her husband to use her son as a man would use a woman rather than endure the duties of a wife.

The killer moved out of the shadows when Clara Mason started down the unlit street. The hunger inside him flared in screaming rage. *His mother!* Her image merged with Clara Mason, making the two of them one.

"You must do this for me!" his mother had demanded, shaking him as she screamed into his face. "You are like him! You must do as he says! You must give him what he wants!"

With her consent, her blessing, his stepfather had led him to the woodshed. First the brute had used the hickory rod. Then he had used the child.

And Clara Mason was the embodiment of his mother.

Moving from shadow to shadow, from tree to tree, he stalked her down the street. His pulse raced as he visualized how he would make her suffer for her devotion—just as he had made his mother suffer for hers. He pictured Clara's face at the end. . . .

Suddenly, unbidden, other faces formed in his mind, those of the two Rangers in town. The Rangers weren't bunglers like Sheriff Whittington; the Rangers were clever—and they were far too close for comfort. Something would have to be done—and quickly—to throw them off his trail.

But what? Could he expect to hide in such a small town? Perhaps he should move on, flee. Maybe he should run to California as he had once fled to Texas. Maybe he could somehow ignore the screaming demand inside him and let Clara Mason live.

Clara Mason. Remembering his prey, he looked for her in the shadowy street and spotted her . . . just as she disappeared into her house. *No!* his mind wailed at him. He had moved too slowly, and now she was lost to him. He couldn't go into her house. It was too dangerous to make a move there, too much chance of being caught. Besides, the Mason home was too close to his secret, his private place.

His gaze shifted from the front door of the Mason house to the small woodshed behind the house. It was there, hidden way in the back of the Reverend Mason's woodshed, that he kept his trophies—just as he had hidden his mother's deaf ears in the woodshed after he had killed her and his stepfather.

It had been a just retribution, almost Biblical in nature. For in the end his mother had finally known the pain that she had inflicted on her son, a son she had allowed to be used in her place.

After killing his stepfather with his own skinning knife, slicing the brute's flesh with the blade as the hickory rod had sliced his own flesh, the killer had entered the house, his clothes drenched in his stepfather's blood. His mother had screamed at the sight, torrential screams that wouldn't cease, but there had been no one to hear—just as no one had heard his screams. First he had used his stepfather's hickory rod on her as it had been used on him countless times, and then he had sliced off her ears as punishment. And when his mother had collapsed on the floor, he had fallen on her with the knife. . . .

He muttered angrily as he abruptly turned from the Mason house. Clara Mason was safe. He could not risk the Rangers coming so close to his secret. The Mason house was, after all, the safest place in all the town. A man of the cloth would never be considered a suspect in the murders—which was why he had chosen the Mason woodshed to hide his trophies in. And that was why Clara Mason was safe this night.

But there would be other nights.

The hunger led him from the Mason home to the heart of San Angelo. He walked through the shadows, an invisible man passing among drunken soldiers. It had been payday, and, as usual, the soldiers were out to blow their monthly wages in one night on whiskey and whores. Even the harlots who peddled their bodies for a few coppers didn't notice the killer, focused as they were on their unmistakable clientele.

His footsteps took him away from the town's lights and toward the shacks and shanties that lined the Concho River. Mexicans and blacks lived there in what was San Angelo's oldest and poorest section. Here, too, lived whores who brought men from the saloons into their own homes to sate carnal lusts for a few nickels and dimes. Two bits was the going rate for a man—white, brown, or black—to fulfill his bestial urges.

The killer watched a tipsy Army private leaving one of the one-room hovels. The soldier turned and dropped a single coin into the hand of the young woman in her early twenties—a half-breed with Negro and Mexican blood in her veins—standing in the doorway.

Waiting until the private disappeared among the shanties, the killer then stepped forward to enter the open doorway of the prostitute's shack. Hearing him enter, the young woman looked up from the table where she sat with a half-filled glass of tequila and a half-burned candle. Her naked body was barely concealed by a sheet loosely draped around it, and at seeing another likely customer, she let the sheet slip, exposing most of a full brown breast.

"You have not brought Rosa any washing to be laundered in the river," she said seductively, a smug smirk poorly disguised as a welcoming smile on her face. "Is it something else you desire of Rosa?"

Closing the door, the killer took a silver dollar from a pocket and held it up. It glinted in the light of the candle. "I believe there are other services you have to offer."

She came to him, letting the sheet drop completely. With her eyes glued to the silver dollar, she didn't see the curved-bladed knife in his hand as he took it from his coat pocket. . . .

He cleaned himself in a washbasin. It was done casually, with no hurry or concern. Rosa was far beyond crying out for help—or crying out for anything else, for that matter.

When the last of her blood was washed away, he tossed the water from the basin out a side window into the dirt. Putting the bowl back on a rough-hewn table beside Rosa's bed, he started for the door. He felt serene. The hunger had been satisfied.

As he approached the door, his gaze lit on a straw basket filled with laundry in a front corner of the room. Rosa hadn't lied when she said she took in washing. But obviously giving pleasure was her main source of income—though she'd been unaware of just how much she'd have to give of herself to earn the silver dollar he had offered. He walked over to the laundry basket and extracted an Army blouse from the pile. His eyes widened at what appeared to be a familiar name sewn inside the collar. Turning to the table, he picked up the candle and held it close to the shirt. It was as he thought. He smiled. *This will do quite nicely,* he told himself as he bundled up the shirt and tucked it under his coat. But that was for future use. Right now he had something else to attend to. He had two more trophies to hide in the oiled leather pouch in Reverend Mason's woodshed.

"I reckon I was wrong about my having the killer locked up in jail," Sheriff Whittington muttered as he covered the bloody remains of Rosa Aguilar with a blanket from her bed. "It looks like one of those seven passengers is our man after all."

A rooster crowed morning as Whittington led Vickery and Cody from the young prostitute's home. He ordered Deputy Todman to bring the undertaker.

Cody pointed to a muddy, reddish patch beside the shanty just under the window. "From the bloody water still in the basin beside the bed and that, it seems that the killer took the time to wash after he killed her."

"With the comin's and goin's in this part of town, there was no need for him to rush," Whittington replied with a disgusted shake of his head. "Nobody notices nothin'—not even a mad-dog butcher walkin' down the street."

"What was left of her blood was dried," Vickery said with a glance back into the house. "That means she'd been dead for hours before her friend who came by to do washin' with her found her. No tellin' what hour she actually died."

The sheriff gazed out at the well-traveled dirt street. "The whoreson's tracks are out there, but there's no way in hell we could ever pick 'em out from all the other footprints."

"No doubt our man knows that," Cody said. "He's learned to hide out in the open—and he's damned good at it. No one even sees him."

Vickery looked up and down the street as though expecting some hitherto unseen trace of the killer to reveal itself. "He's seen all right," the captain growled. "He's just not noticed. He moves through this town as conspicuous as you please. He fits right in; he doesn't stand out."

"That could describe any of the six men on that stage," Whittington said. "Most men in town have paid a visit to the women here at one time or another. Hell, even Reverend Mason comes down here regularly—though not for the same reasons. He and his wife try to help the sick and ailin' while preachin' the Good Book on the side."

Whittington paused to scratch the stubble on his neck. Like Cody and Vickery, he'd been awakened with the news of yet another murder, and he had dressed and come directly to the shack without shaving. "Hell, the only one who might open eyes around here is Leslie Wakefield. You don't see too many schoolmarms down in this section of town."

An idea wiggled free from the back of Cody's mind. Why hadn't he thought of it before? "Unless Leslie Wakefield was dressed as a man."

"Impossible! She's far too . . . well, normal," Whittington insisted.

"I'll agree that it seems unlikely, but we know we're dealing with a very cunning—and very mad—individual here. Which means we can't rule out anything. Or anyone."

The sheriff could offer no argument to that; still, his expression was one of discomfort with the idea. "So, where do we go from here?"

"We do like we agreed to earlier," the captain answered. "Question our seven passengers, trading off the names we had yesterday. Cody'll take mine, you take his, and I'll take yours. And we talk to 'em now while the day's still new. One of those seven is a killer, and we want to make him think we're walkin' in his footsteps only an inch or two off his heels. That should make him nervous . . . and nervous men make mistakes."

Cody arrived at Leslie Wakefield's house just as she was stepping out the front door. The freshly painted white cottage with its white picket fence and garden was no doubt part of the inducement that had brought the pretty young Arkansas schoolteacher to San Angelo. Opening the gate, the Ranger greeted the young woman with a tip of his hat, then introduced himself.

Leslie shifted the books and brass bell she held from one arm to another. "Another Texas Ranger? I just spoke with a Captain Vickery yesterday."

"I know, ma'am," Cody said, offering no apology or explanation. "But I'd like to talk with you this morning."

"I have to ring the bell in twenty minutes. If you don't mind walking to the school with me, we can talk. It's only a half mile or so up the road." The schoolteacher looked thoughtful. "I assume this is about the murders Captain Vickery mentioned yesterday."

"There was another one last night," Cody said, going straight to the heart of the matter. "A young woman on the other side of town was killed in her own house."

Leslie Wakefield stopped abruptly. Her rosy cheeks paled. "Was she killed in the same manner as the others?"

"I'm afraid so. I'm also afraid I have to ask you where you were last night."

The schoolteacher drew a breath and nodded. "After school yesterday I came home to prepare my dinner. That was when Captain Vickery visited me. When he left, I ate my meal. Usually I would have begun preparing today's lessons, but I was invited to a meeting of the women's auxiliary at the church last night. I attended with Clara Mason, the minister's wife. The meeting lasted until nine o'clock or so."

Nine o'clock left more than enough time for her to have committed the young prostitute's murder, Cody thought, in light of what he had learned a short while earlier. One of Rosa's neighbors had come to the sheriff's office to report that he had seen Rosa standing in her doorway and bidding a black customer farewell—"He was picking up his laundry, señor," the man had insisted—after eleven.

"After that where did you go?" Cody asked Leslie.

"Well, nine is generally late for me," she replied. "I wanted to return home immediately and go to bed. However, three of the women at the meeting convinced me that I could be of help at a quilting bee. You see, a flash flood a month ago washed away three homes here in San

Angelo. The men in the church are rebuilding those homes, and the women in the auxiliary are sewing quilts for those families. Winter isn't that far away. It was a little after midnight when I finally returned home. Mr. Wilson and his wife, Ruth, escorted me. They said that with these brutal murders it wasn't safe for a woman to be alone at night on the streets."

"A sensible strategy," Cody said. He asked her for the names of the other women who participated in the quilting bee, and she willingly gave them.

They had reached the schoolhouse, and the young teacher turned to the Ranger. "Now, Mr. Cody, if you'll excuse me, I must call my pupils to school. It wouldn't do for a new teacher to be tardy herself during her first week of classes," she said with a smile.

Cody smiled in return. "Of course. And thanks for your help."

He turned and headed back for the center of town. He'd check out Leslie Wakefield's story, of course, both the auxiliary meeting and the quilting bee. If the other women verified her attendance at each, he'd go find the next suspect on his list—the man at the top of the sheriff's list—Wilson Cutter.

It was Cutter who found him. When Cody had checked the gambler's room in a hotel down the street from the Three Rivers One, he'd been out. The Ranger left a message for Cutter with the desk clerk, saying that he wanted to talk with him, then returned to his own hotel for breakfast. The waiter had just placed a plate heaped high with ham and eggs before Cody when Cutter pushed through the saloon's batwings.

"If you're a Texas Ranger named Sam Cody, I'm Wilson Cutter," the gambler said as he stepped to the table and seated himself without waiting for an invitation. "I understand you want to talk with me."

"I'm Cody, and you're right. I want to talk to you." Cody blew across his steaming cup of coffee, then added, "You were out and about early this morning."

"So were you, I hear." The gambler waved for a cup of coffee. "Rumor about town says there was another murder last night."

If the plaid-suited tinhorn had expected to take Cody by surprise with his knowledge, it didn't work. "Where were you last night?"

"Thought that might be what you wanted to talk to me about," Cutter said, grinning like the cat who'd just gotten the canary. "I was busy making myself a fat grubstake until the wee hours of the morning, Ranger. Found myself a nice little poker game down at the Two Sisters Saloon and came away with three hundred dollars in my pocket." He chuckled. "Five cowboys from the Crooked J Ranch will be certain to remember me. In fact, I doubt they'll ever be able to forget me."

Cutter's cocksure attitude grated on Cody like a rasp on wood. But an attitude, good or bad, didn't make a man a killer. "Give me their names, and I'll check and see just how much they remember."

Cutter did, then asked, "Anything else, Ranger? If not, I'm going to do myself some shopping for a good horse this morning."

"Thinking about leaving town?" Cody stared across the table at the gambler.

"Yep. Maybe heading to El Paso or up to Santa Fe," Cutter answered. "There's plenty of games here in San Angelo, but the stakes aren't big enough. Back on the river, last night's game would have brought in three thousand, not just three hundred."

Cody didn't care about poker winnings; he wanted to make certain Cutter didn't suddenly vanish. "I'd get any idea of traveling on out of my head if I was you. There's a sheriff and two Texas Rangers in this town who wouldn't look kindly on you just up and pulling out of San Angelo. Fact is, that'd be the kind of move that might make 'em think you were the man going around cutting folks up."

Cutter's cocksure smile transformed into an expression of indignity. "Are you saying I'm under arrest?"

"Nope." Cody sopped up the last of the egg yolk with a piece of biscuit and popped it in his mouth, then chewed

with great deliberation before swallowing. He took pleasure
in annoying Cutter with this punctilious action. "I'm saying
Sheriff Whittington would be glad to find you accommoda-
tions over at his jail should you decide to leave town," he
finally added.

"You can't do that! I haven't broken any law!" Cutter's
indignity rose to outrage. "This might be Texas, but it's still
America. You can't throw a man in jail for no reason!"

Cody shrugged. "I'd consider any attempt to leave town
as interference with a Ranger investigation. That's good
enough to get you a free room in the jail. But I reckon as
how you and a judge might disagree with my legal call, so
you'll eventually get your day in court and be free to ride
out of here."

"Eventually?"

"When the circuit judge comes through." Cody took
a long, leisurely sip of his coffee. "That's four times a
year, once each quarter. He was through not long ago,
from what I understand, so if I figure right he'll be back
through around the first of December—or maybe January
if his docket's heavy in other towns."

Cutter's dark eyes met Cody's for several seconds.
"You're serious, aren't you?"

"Serious as the day is long—or months, as the case may
be," Cody said. "Go ahead and buy yourself a horse, Cutter.
Just don't get on him."

"You—" Cutter swallowed whatever curse was forming
as he pushed from the table. He glared at the Ranger for
several seconds, then pivoted sharply and stormed from the
saloon.

Cody returned to his coffee. He'd find Vickery or
Whittington and warn them they might have a bird trying
to take wing. Then he'd ride out and talk with the five
cowboys who supposedly had played poker with Cutter
last night.

He groaned inwardly. It was going to be a long, hard
day.

CHAPTER 10

Captain Vickery lit the oil lamp in his room, then closed the door. Outside in the hallway he heard Cody's door closing, and he wondered if the younger Ranger was as bewildered by the case as he was. Sam Cody was a hard man to judge. He didn't complain, he didn't brag. He just went about his business until a job was done.

Vickery couldn't help but wonder when *this* job would be done.

He walked over to the bed and sat down on the edge. Sighing heavily, he pulled off his boots, slipped out of his coat and vest, then loosened his string tie and opened a collar button. He glanced at the bed's two pillows. As tired as he was, he knew sleep wouldn't come easy. He'd just keep turning over and over like the thoughts in his mind kept turning over and over.

He padded over to the window and opened it, then looked down on the street. Light glared from San Angelo's saloons and houses of ill repute. Somehow it didn't surprise him that a mad butcher had found his way to this hellhole. Right at this moment San Angelo reminded him of the Biblical Sodom and Gomorrah. Except the Lord hadn't sent two angels down to wipe San Angelo off the face of the earth; the state of Texas had sent two Rangers to apprehend a bloody murderer.

But Rangers were a far cry from angels, Vickery reflected as he pulled a chair in front of the window and sat down to enjoy the cool night breeze. Rangers were flesh-and-blood men, and though Vickery viewed them as being on the side of the Lord, they sorely lacked divine guidance. The best they could do was muddle through.

Vickery felt as though he'd muddled his way through a mountain of manure today, and all for nothing. Despite all the questioning he and Cody and Whittington had done, they were no closer to the killer than they'd been two days before. All seven of their suspects had alibis—good, solid alibis.

The captain looked over at the jail. Even it was empty tonight. After last night's murder Whittington could no longer hold his drifters behind bars. Even he had admitted it was impossible for a jailed man to have committed the last killing.

But which of the seven had taken a knife and sliced open that young prostitute? Vickery felt certain the key to the killer's identity was staring him in the face, but he just couldn't see it. Or maybe he was just an old man fooling himself.

There was nothing more he could do but wait until the killer made the next move. And Vickery knew all too well what that move would be.

Cody, too, dragged a chair in front of the open window, relishing the cool breeze on his naked chest. His body felt like a rock that had baked in the sun from morning to sunset, and now that darkness had come, it was releasing all the heat it had stored during the day. It might be October, but it sure felt like the early, hot days of a Texas September.

The Ranger watched the ranch hands and soldiers sauntering along the street as they sought out the pleasures so openly available in San Angelo. Somewhere out there was a killer. Each day that passed better illustrated the fact that this maniac was totally, frighteningly different from any of the hardcases and owlhoots he had ever come up against.

Even a man with the soul of a saint could understand the temptation that sometimes seduced someone to rustle steers or deal from the bottom of the deck or rob a bank. Quick, easy cash was always waiting to lure a teetering or desperate man over the line that separated good folks from outlaws.

Hate was something else that was elemental, driving many a man to put a bullet into an enemy. In the days before Cody had first pinned on a sheriff's badge in El Paso, he'd lived close to hate, trodding a path along that line himself. One misstep might have landed his face on a wanted poster.

Sure, Cody had stared into the eyes of men who seemed to relish killing, feeling no guilt in the taking of another life. They were rare, but they did exist, and they were far more deadly than a rattler. But this killer was beyond his grasp. He couldn't conceive of what force drove a man—or a woman—to slaughter and carve open another human being like some animal ready to be cleaned and dressed.

Some men, usually professional shooters, killed for the sake of reputation or notoriety. But even that wasn't the case here. No one knew the killer, and except for a few paragraphs in the local weekly paper mentioning the killer's three victims, the bodies left strewn from Texarkana to San Angelo had received no publicity.

Was it some ungodly pleasure that drove the killer? If it were, it was something so dark, so alien, that Cody couldn't begin to understand. One of seven passengers who had been aboard that stage was the killer. Every single one of those seven appeared to be completely ordinary. But in one of them something evil hid deep within the soul, something that could be concealed until a blade was drawn and used.

Damn! Cody's mind railed. What *was* that something! What could turn an ordinary man or woman into a butcher of his own kind? If he could find that something, he would find the killer.

A cold shiver that had nothing to do with the breeze shot up his spine and sent gooseflesh rippling over his body. The only way another man could ever understand what drove this bloody bastard was to actually live in the killer's head, where the dark secret dwelled. And that was something Cody had no desire to find out.

Casting aside that thought, the Ranger focused again on the street below. He recalled the discussion held outside the prostitute's shanty in the Mexican section of San Angelo: The killer's presence in the town was so accepted that he moved through the night completely unnoticed. He was part of the background rather than the center of attention.

Not at all like Lisa Kingston, the Ranger thought with a smile. The young woman had just exited a seamstress shop half a block up the street and was holding a paper-wrapped bundle in her arms. This time, rather than jeans, shirt, and boots, the auburn-haired beauty wore a yellow-and-white striped dress—one, Cody thought, more appropriate for a summer day than an autumn night. On the other hand, he reminded himself, tonight's heat belonged to summer rather than fall.

He watched Lisa cross the boardwalk and climb into a one-horse buggy, glimpsing a flourish of white petticoats about her ankles as she did so. In pants or dress Lisa Kingston was quite an eyeful, the kind of woman that set a man's mind wandering and wondering.

Cody chuckled ruefully. Wondering was about all he'd ever do when it came to Lisa Kingston. The young woman's sharp, biting tongue had made it clear that she had no use for lawmen unable to bring in her father's killer. And he couldn't actually blame her.

Lisa lifted her reins and got the buggy swung around, and Cody shifted his attention back to the street. Feeling like a member of the audience at a play, he shifted his focus from the actors—the cowboys and the soldiers—to the backdrops. His gaze ran over the buildings, their lit windows, their open doorways. He searched for the ordinary, the unnoticed.

Stroking his thick mustache, Cody thought how the town had a whole host of invisible people. There at one corner two men leaned against a saloon wall, talking. They were commonplace; their actions were usual; the eye simply passed over them.

Across the street in a second-story window of another hotel, a woman sat watching the street below just as Cody was doing. How long had she been there? He hadn't noticed her before. Did she see him, or was he one of the invisible people to her?

And that man dressed in a black suit and straight-brimmed hat seated on a barrel in the alley beside the dressmaker's shop. How long had he been there? Cody wondered as he watched the man stand when Lisa Kingston drove by. For the first time the Ranger understood how the killer had moved through this town and all the other towns so easily. At this distance Cody couldn't even be certain whether the wiry-looking figure was truly a man or a woman dressed as a man. Even when the man stepped onto the boardwalk and watched Lisa depart, he appeared to be no more than a background shadow.

Cody's heart pounded with excitement. He hadn't found the key to unlock the killer's identity, but he now under-stood how the killer worked and moved. And that was more than he'd known before sitting at the window and observing.

Questioning the seven passengers wasn't going to pro-duce results. They had to be stalked the way the killer stalked his victims. That meant working at night, fading into the background, and following each one of the seven. Since this killer was like no other he'd run into, the method needed to capture him would be like no other Cody had ever employed.

In fact, the Ranger realized, Vickery and he shouldn't be the ones to employ them. In all likelihood the killer was alert to the five lawmen in San Angelo. What was needed was new pairs of eyes to watch from the back-ground, people the killer wouldn't suspect were watch-ing him.

What with the rest of Company C probably still out on patrol, Cody doubted that Captain Vickery would wire Del Rio for other Rangers. But maybe Whittington knew some men in town who could be trusted and would be willing to take on the job of watching the suspects night after night until the killer revealed himself.

A weight lifted from the Ranger's shoulders. He was certain he'd found the solution. He pulled his watch from his pocket and opened it. It was late, but he'd chance Vickery's wrath for waking him. This was too important to wait for morning. It was time to get the wheels turning if they were to stop the killer before he claimed another victim.

Slipping the timepiece back into his pocket, Cody stood and began buttoning his shirt, idly watching out the window. His fingers froze at the last button. Something was wrong, though he couldn't pin down just what it was.

Below, the man in black stood staring down the road that Lisa Kingston had taken. He then stepped to the hitchrack, where three horses were tethered. Looking around surreptitiously, as though to make certain he went unwatched, the man then made his move. He selected the middle horse, untied its reins, mounted, and rode in the direction Lisa had gone, keeping the horse at an easy jog.

Fear gripped Cody. He knew beyond a shadow of a doubt that the man in black was the killer. *The man was the killer, and Lisa Kingston was his next intended victim.*

Cody snatched his holstered Colt from the bedpost and buckled it to his waist as he ran from the room into the hallway. He hammered a fist on Vickery's door, shouting, "Cap'n, wake up! I'm certain I've spotted the killer, and he's right now following Lisa Kingston home! I'm going after him!"

Cody was halfway down the stairs when he heard a sleepy Vickery call out, "What did you say?"

"The killer's after Lisa Kingston!" Cody shouted back without breaking his stride.

He darted out of the hotel and stopped on the boardwalk, looking south. The man in black was nowhere to be seen. Cody was about to race for the livery stable, where his horse was boarded, when he noticed a saddled gray gelding tied at the hitching rail. Without hesitation, he untied the horse's reins and swung into the saddle. The horse's angry owner came out of the hotel, shouting for Cody to stop. Cody shouted back that he was a Ranger, not a horse thief, and it was a dire emergency. Slamming his spurs into the horse's sides, he wheeled the animal around and raced south.

Within minutes he was beyond the lights of San Angelo. He looked all around but saw nothing except the moonlit, shadowy countryside. Cody suspected that the killer would circle ahead of Lisa, then wait for her to come to him. The Ranger imagined a dozen scenarios that could play the unsuspecting young woman directly into the killer's hands—like lying in her path as though he were injured, and when Lisa stopped to assist him, repaying her kindness with steel.

Frantic, Cody jabbed his heels into the gray's flanks to urge the horse to greater speed. He had to reach Lisa before she reached the waiting killer. Cody lashed the horse with the ends of the reins, and the gray bounded forward.

A mile, maybe a mile and a half, from the outskirts of San Angelo, Cody spotted the slow-moving buggy.

"Miss Kingston! Miss Kingston!" he called.

The buggy continued to roll forward.

"Miss Kingston, stop!" Cody shouted at the top of his lungs. "Miss Kingston, it's Sam Cody. Stop! You're in danger!"

He barely discerned a pale blur as Lisa's head poked briefly around the buggy's top to look back at him. Then she faced forward again and drew her horse to a halt. Cody caught up with her.

"Mr. Cody?" Lisa asked, staring up at him. "What's wrong?"

Cody suddenly realized that he had ridden after the woman on no more than a gut feeling that the man in black was a killer and that Lisa Kingston might well think him crazy. He didn't care.

"I happened to be looking out my window when you left the seamstress shop, and I saw a man ride out after you. I'm certain it's the killer."

"The killer?" Her expression was hard to discern in the shadows cast by the moon, but Cody had no trouble recognizing the incredulity in her voice. "What makes you think it was the killer?"

"A feeling—something about the way he watched you leave town. I couldn't risk being wrong. I figured it was better to come up the fool than have your body found tomorrow morning." He chuckled dryly. "Though the man I 'borrowed' this horse from might not necessarily agree."

For a moment Lisa studied him; then she said, "I would be tempted to wonder if perhaps you had something else on your mind—except I don't imagine you would steal a horse just to ride after me to get to know me better."

Cody grinned. "Well, I wouldn't steal a horse to do it, but I wouldn't mind getting to know you better."

"You're serious about this feeling, aren't you?" Lisa asked, her tone suddenly far more solemn.

"Dead serious." Cody's gaze swept the countryside. He saw nothing. "Serious enough for me to escort you home, just to be on the safe side."

Lisa shook her head. "I don't think that will be necessary, Mr. Cody. I keep a loaded Winchester under this seat. And I know how to use it."

Cody was in no mood to argue. He was going to accompany her home whether she liked it or not. He said coolly, "A rifle's only good when you see danger coming. Remember, your pa was toting a weapon when he was killed. It didn't do him any good."

Lisa gasped, though whether surprised by the Ranger's harsh comparison or in fear, Cody didn't know—but she gave in. "I guess it wouldn't hurt to have company."

"Wouldn't hurt at all," Cody agreed.

She slapped the reins to her horse's back and the buggy trundled forward.

As they rode slowly along, the Ranger looked around the surrounding terrain. Plains of low rolling hills stretched in all directions, broken in the distant west by a pair of conical mountains and a line of hogback ridges running northward. Except for a copse of gnarled old mesquite trees that they were approaching, there was nothing but grassland waving in the moonlight. Or so it appeared. But the killer was a master of invisibility. It wasn't far from this point that Calvin Kingston, Lisa's father, had been murdered three nights before. And the moon had been a lot brighter then.

Cody examined the countryside with a new eye for detail. A rolling plain was never as open as it appeared. The Comanche had known that all too well. Gullies and depressions in the earth could easily hide a man and horse. And at night a crouched man might appear to be no more than a dense clump of weeds or a dark patch of ground. Darkness played strange tricks on a man's eyes. The man in black probably knew that and used it to his advantage.

Cody rested his hand lightly on the grip of his Colt. The killer had tried for two victims at once in Eldorado. He might well try again tonight. If, as Cody was certain, the man in black was the murderer, Cody was also certain that he was up ahead somewhere—waiting, watching, calculating how he'd kill two rather than one.

But where? Where was the bloody bastard hiding? Cody scanned the moonlit terrain once more. He saw dozens of places that could conceal a man on a horse and twice as many where a man on foot might hide. His gaze returned to the twisted mesquites rising a hundred yards down the wheel-rutted road.

The sound of approaching hooves snapped the Ranger's head around. His hand tightened around the Colt's grip.

"Cody!" Captain Vickery's familiar voice hailed. "Cody, hold up!"

Cody brought the gray to a halt, and Lisa pulled back on her reins. "It's the captain," Cody explained. "I told him to follow me."

Lisa looked up at Cody. "Two Texas Rangers to escort one woman? I feel honored—though I believe you're wasting your time."

Vickery reined in a black mare that Cody hadn't seen before. "I hope you know what you're doin', Cody," the older Ranger muttered. "I grabbed the first horse I saw when I came out of the hotel."

"That means you're *both* horse thieves," Lisa said wryly.

Ignoring the sardonic remark, Cody told Vickery what he had witnessed from his hotel window. "I know I'm basing this on just a hunch, but I'm certain that the man in black is our killer."

"Well, Cody, your hunches have proved right before, so I won't tell you otherwise," Vickery said. Suddenly the captain twisted his head from side to side, and he sniffed the air like a hound picking up a scent. "You smell somethin' on the breeze? It ain't there all the time. Just somethin' kinda sweet under the dust. It comes and goes. Can't place it, though."

"Yes, I smell it!" Lisa exclaimed, sniffing deeply herself. "It's like the scent of some flower. But that doesn't make sense—it's October, and all the wildflowers have long since faded." She sniffed again. "I *know* that smell. But it's too faint to recognize. It's definitely perfumey, though."

Cody inhaled three times before he caught the scent wafting on the breeze. As Lisa had said, it was a perfumed scent.

Vickery eased back his coat to reveal his own Colt. "I don't know what that smell is, but it don't belong."

Cody looked around the countryside once more, his gaze alighting on the mesquites. Indicating the copse of trees with his chin, he said softly, "I think someone might be waiting for us up ahead. The wind's coming out of the south."

Vickery's head turned toward the mesquites. His eyes narrowed. "I suppose we ought to go take us a look-see."

The killer knew he had to flee the instant the two riders angled their mounts toward the mesquites. Yanking on the reins, he whipped the bay around and slammed his heels into the horse's flanks.

"There he is!" came a shout on the breeze.

"I see the demon spawn!" came a second voice. "Don't let him get far ahead or we'll lose him!"

The Rangers! The killer recognized their voices. His temples pounded as though they were going to explode. He should have guessed the riders' identities sooner, but the gnawing hunger inside had made him lose all sense of caution.

Sucking down the panic that swirled in his brain, the killer spurred his mount on.

As the bay bounded through the tall grass, the killer realized that running was no good. There was only open ground. He'd be too easy to spot. He had to find a solution.

His heels whipped into the bay. The animal lunged forward with greater speed. The killer then kicked free of the stirrups and threw himself from the saddle.

He relied on the dense grass to break his fall. It did. Still he gritted his teeth to hold back a loud grunt as he spilled to the ground onto his back. He rolled for several yards, then stopped, lying unmoving and listening to the fleeing hooves of the bay. From behind he heard the Rangers. They were fast approaching.

"I lost the bastard!" The voice belonged to the younger one, the man called Sam Cody. "The grass is too tall, and the moon isn't bright enough."

Then the older one, Captain Vickery, answered. "I hear him. Swing to the right! He's ridin' east!"

Their mounts' hoofbeats grew closer and closer. For an instant the killer feared the two Rangers would ride directly over him. But they passed to his right, heading after the riderless horse.

The killer rose to his knees and crouched. He briefly considered returning to the young woman in the buggy. What a triumph to take her life force while the Rangers searched for him!

Then reason prevailed.

Turning toward the river, he pushed his way through the thick grass, his movements hidden by the night. The hunger was subsiding. Besides, he had a surprise to prepare for the Rangers back in town. The Army blouse was hidden in his secret place. He would use it to throw the Rangers off his trail. He would use it to make them utter laughingstocks. He would use it to make them doubt their competence and judgment till their dying day.

He would teach them to interfere. . . .

With Captain Vickery leading the riderless bay, the two Rangers quickly returned to where Lisa Kingston waited in her buggy.

"He got away from us," Vickery growled disgustedly as he drew up beside the young woman. "He set his horse free, and we took the bait like rank amateurs and chased a wild goose."

Cody shifted in his saddle and looked over his shoulder. "Odds are he made a beeline to the river and is back in town by now. Like as not he's holed up safe and sound in his own bed, laughing at us."

"Could be," Vickery replied. "But this one don't think like an ordinary hombre. Could be all we did was make him as mad as a nest of wasps. He might've decided to wait up ahead and try for Miss Kingston again."

Vickery turned to the young woman. "I suggest you let Cody escort you back to your ranch. I really don't think you can expect more trouble, but I'd feel better if Cody was with you."

Those were exactly Cody's plans, but it made things easier to have the captain's approval. No sense taking chances.

"What about you, Captain?" Lisa asked.

Vickery nodded at the horse he was leading. "I'm goin' back into town. This here cayuse just might take me to the man who rode him. No need waitin' till mornin' to find out."

"Cap'n, he might be waiting somewhere on the road back to town." Cody didn't mention Vickery's first run-in with the killer, but it sat heavily on his mind.

"I've thought of that, too." The Ranger captain pulled his big Colt from its holster. "This'll keep me company into San Angelo. I suggest you do the same till you meet me back at the sheriff's office."

Nodding, Cody eased out his Frontier Colt. "I'll be back as soon as I see Miss Kingston home."

"I'll be waitin' for you." Vickery reined the black mare toward the lights of San Angelo. "Hopefully we'll have the owner of the bay behind bars when you get back."

Cody nudged the gray forward as Lisa popped the reins onto the back of her own horse. The buggy creaked as it rolled forward.

Several minutes passed, and then Lisa turned to the Ranger. "Mr. Cody, I feel that I owe you an apology."

"Just Cody will do," he said. His gaze never strayed from searching the land ahead. "And why do you owe me an apology?"

"For what I said earlier," she replied in a voice filled with awkwardness. "I thought you were acting like a fool, riding after me on a hunch. Obviously I was wrong. I'm sorry."

"No need to be. I could just as likely have been wrong," he answered. "In truth, I wish I had been. I don't like the idea of him coming after you."

Lisa rode silently for a half mile before asking, "Why me? Does he have something against Kingstons?"

Cody slowly shook his head. "I don't think so. I think it was probably just a case of being in the wrong place at the right time. You know, your leaving town when you did made you a convenient target. But on the other hand you might frighten him."

"*Me* frighten *him?*" Lisa's tone was incredulous. "I haven't stopped shaking since you found him hiding in those mesquites. But exactly what do you mean?"

"Well, you've made your plans to bring in someone else on this case well known in town. It could be that that set him off. Our man doesn't like strangers with faces he doesn't know. An invisible man doesn't like to have one of his own kind on his heels."

"Invisible man?" Lisa looked up at the Ranger questioningly. "What are you talking about?"

Cody explained what had come to him while sitting at the hotel window, concluding, "He knows Cap'n Vickery and me as well as Sheriff Whittington and his deputies. He can keep an eye peeled for us and know if we're on his tail. But you want to bring in someone he doesn't know— an invisible man after an invisible man."

"Then I was right about getting outside help," Lisa said.

"Partly. One man won't be enough, though. We need seven new pairs of eyes to keep watch on everybody who came in on that stage. I have a couple of plans in mind that I'll discuss with Cap'n Vickery to come up with the men needed for the task. There's a gallows waiting for the man in black, and he's a lot closer to it than he realizes. I just hope we can get him before he kills again."

The rutted road wound between two grassy hills that opened onto a draw stretching for miles. The Kingston ranch house sat in the middle of that draw.

"We're here," Lisa said, a sigh of relief in her voice as they pulled up to the front gate. "I think I'm safe now."

"I'd feel better if I checked out the house before I headed back," Cody said.

He received no protest from the young woman.

The Ranger dismounted and entered the front door first, gun drawn. Lisa stepped in behind him, lit a lamp near the door, and handed it to him. With his Colt in his right hand and the lamp in his left, Cody cautiously moved through the six-room house. All the rooms were empty.

"I reckon it's another case of being safe rather than sorry," he said when he returned to the open front door. He nodded toward the bunkhouse, adding, "I think it'd be best if I got one of the hands to stand guard outside the house tonight."

Lisa shook her head as she took the lamp and placed it back on the table. "The ranch isn't that big. We only hire on hands for branding and at roundup. I'll be all right by myself. There are two shotguns in my father's den. I'll load one and keep it by my bed tonight."

"And secure your door and windows," Cody suggested.

"I will."

Without warning, Lisa took a step closer to Cody and threw her arms around him, pressing against him. She rose on her tiptoes, her mouth seeking and finding his. Cody reacted as any man would who suddenly found a beautiful young woman kissing him: His arms encircled her slender waist, and he returned the kiss with as much passion as Lisa displayed.

Sooner than the Ranger would've liked, Lisa's lips slipped from his. She stepped back and stared unashamedly into his eyes. "Thank you, Cody. I guess I wouldn't be standing here if it hadn't been for you."

Cody grinned, still savoring the feel of her mouth on his. Her kiss had held more than a simple thank you; it had spoken of silent promises. But those promises would have to wait. For now he was needed back in town.

"It was my pleasure," he told her. "I'd better be heading back now. You be careful tonight—and keep that scattergun near."

"I will. And, Cody, *you* be careful. I think I've grown to like having a Texas Ranger escort."

His grin widened. "I'll do that." He turned and walked to his waiting mount. So far it had been a hell of a night, filled with more than one surprise—and sunup was still a long way off.

CHAPTER
|||||||||||||||||||||||||||| **11** ||||||||||||||||||||||||||||

This time there were tracks. But what few prints there were led into the river and could have belonged to anyone wearing boots. And a search of the mesquite copse provided nothing but facefuls of spines that stung like the bite of red ants.

Cody had recognized the futility of the search a full hour before Sheriff Whittington called it off. The search had brought them no closer to the killer than the bay recovered last night had, since—as Cody and Vickery had done—the killer had "borrowed" the horse from the hitching rail in front of the saloon. While Vickery and Cody had been out on the trail chasing after the man in black, the horse's owner had been in Whittington's office reporting the horse's theft.

"Any new ideas on what to do next?" Whittington asked the two Rangers as they walked to their horses tied under the mesquites. "What about Cody's idea of spying on the seven?"

"I think Cody's got the right idea," Vickery said. "Can you get seven men ready by tonight?"

Cody didn't know if the two older lawmen actually found merit in his suggestion or if they were merely desperate and willing to give anything a try.

"Not by tonight, but I should be able to get the men I want together by tomorrow," Whittington replied. "One of them's named Ellis. He's a local rancher who wore my badge for a month before I took the job. He's up in Abilene on business at the moment, but I understand he'll be home by tomorrow."

"*Andrew* Ellis?" Vickery asked as he climbed into the saddle.

"That's right. You know him?"

"We served together out of San Antonio in a Ranger company before the war of northern aggression. Andy's a good man."

"Then we'll wait until tomorrow to do anything more," Whittington said.

Cody spoke up. "I think that'd be a wrong move. We should keep doing what we've been doing. If we let up, the killer will get wise to the fact that something else is in the wind. We've got to keep our new men invisible by the five of us being as visible as possible. If the killer's watching *us*, he's less apt to notice the new men watching *him*."

Vickery nodded his approval. "Cody's right. We can't let on that anythin's changed, or our spies won't be able to do their job. So we continue questionin' the seven just like we've been doin'."

Seven divided by three meant two with one left over. It was Cody's turn to draw that extra one. Lewis Jessup was the first on his list, and it was the rancher who now laughed in response to Cody's inquiry as to his whereabouts the night before.

"I'm sorry, Ranger. I know this is a serious matter—a damned serious matter—but you have to see it through my eyes," Jessup said.

"I'm listening," Cody responded gruffly.

"Well, first there was Sheriff Whittington, then your Captain Vickery, and now you. All three of you rode out here wantin' to know where I was the night before or when I was last in town," Jessup said, still chuckling. "Ranger, I'm a family man with eight young 'uns. And I don't run a big spread here. I got my hands full just keepin' food on the table for all those mouths. And believe me, they're hungry mouths. Hell's bells, friend, Cora and me're lucky if we can get the family gathered up for a ride into town once or twice a month."

Cody understood the hardships of ranching and large families. He also understood the bodies the killer left wherever he trod. "And last night?"

Jessup pushed away from the hitching rail he leaned on and called into the ranch house behind him. "Cora, darlin', come on out here a minute. And bring the twins with you. There's a man here who wants to know where I was last night."

A plump woman in her early thirties appeared in the doorway. She carried two infants no older than six months in her arms.

"Cora, this here's another Texas Ranger, name of Cody. Mr. Cody rode all the way out from town to ask where I was last night."

"Why, Lew was here with me and the kids." She shifted from one foot to the other to keep the double burden in her arms balanced. "We was up most of the night with these two. They had a touch of the colic. Kept the whole house up with their bawlin'."

The Ranger smiled, understanding now Lewis Jessup's unexpected initial response. Cody had to admit there was a shade of humor in suspecting a man of murder when he'd in fact been up all night tending children with ailing bowels. "Thank you, Mrs. Jessup." He looked back at Lewis Jessup and grinned. "I reckon you *did* have your hands full last night."

Jessup broke out in laughter again. "Full to overflowin' at times, you might say."

Harry Farris answered Cody's question with a wide sweep of his arm around the dry-goods store. "I was here well into the night. Early morning, actually. Taking inventory. Christmas is coming on us fast. I need to make certain I'm stocked for the holiday season. A man in my business can make a tidy sum come the holidays. That is, if he's got the items his customers want."

The merchant stood behind the counter of his store and looked Cody right in the eye. "This year I'll be offering pianos and organs. They're high-dollar items, but I'm hoping to sell a few. Quite a number of the ladies in town are musical, you know."

The Ranger cared little about the musical abilities of San Angelo's residents. "Is there anyone who can verify that you were in the store?"

"My clerk, Toby, was here with me every minute." Farris indicated a man who was brushing a feather duster over the shelves that lined the opposite wall of the store. "That's Toby over there. Ask him what we were doing last night, if you want."

Cody did. The clerk confirmed Farris's alibi in a sour voice that said he had hated every moment of the inventory check that had lasted until two A.M.

Thanking the two men, the Ranger left the store. He stood on the boardwalk out front and rubbed a weary hand over his neck. His third day of questioning the passengers was proving to be as fruitless as the first two.

"Ranger, I know you've got a job to do, but so do I," Clayton Partee said, his hands resting on the saddle horn as he stared fixedly across a draw containing five hundred head of longhorns. "I'm a rancher, but I'm also a businessman. And I've got a reputation to maintain. It doesn't look good to the community to have some lawman come chasing me down every other day. I handle a lot of government contracts for both beeves and horses. I wouldn't want any official getting the notion that I might not be operating on the up and up."

"Like you said," Cody responded, "I've got a job to do. And I *will* do it. I'm sorry if my doing that job inconveniences you, but I can show you three fresh graves in San Angelo of people who have been inconvenienced far more than you."

It was evident from the young rancher's stiff face, even in profile, that he didn't care for that answer, but he kept his mouth shut. For that Cody was thankful. He had no more liking for this part of his job than those being questioned did.

"Now, what about last night?" he asked.

"I was over at Fort Concho, the dinner guest of Captain Thomas Harrington," Partee answered, his attention still glued to the cowpunchers working the herd.

"I've met Cap'n Harrington," Cody said. "I'll talk with him to verify your story."

"You do that, Ranger," Partee said, finally turning to look at Cody. "And while you're at it, you can also verify that after dinner I played poker with Harrington and five junior officers. I lost heavily. I usually do when I play with Army officers. It makes for friendly relations with the boys in blue, if you get my drift."

Before Cody could form another question in his mind, Partee added, "Now, you've done your job. If you don't mind, I'd like to get on with mine."

Not waiting for a response, he tapped his mount's sides with his spurs and rode down the slight rise to join the herd.

For a moment Cody stared after him. The man's arrogance seemed to be a common trait of Texas's new breed of ranchers. The Ranger didn't like it, but that was no reason to ride after Partee and continue the questioning. As much as Cody would've enjoyed inconveniencing him, there wasn't time. It was a long ride back into town. And Cody did intend to talk to Captain Harrington about his dinner guest last night.

When Sheriff Whittington heard his office door open that evening, he swiveled around in his chair. Seeing who his visitor was, he frowned. "Young lady, the last thing I need today is you criticizin' me. If you ain't got nothin' good to say, then just turn yourself about and walk on outta here."

Lisa Kingston came to an abrupt halt with one foot over the threshold, her eyes wide and her mouth open.

"I believe Miss Kingston just stopped by to say hello," Cody said, pushing from his chair and crossing to the door.

"I asked her to last night. I wanted to make certain she didn't have any trouble after I left her ranch."

Taking the young woman's arm, the Ranger escorted her back outside and closed the door behind him.

"Actually, I wanted to find out if any progress has been made," Lisa said, her green eyes darting between the sheriff's office and Cody. "But I also wanted to thank you and your captain again for what you did last night."

Cody glanced through the window at Vickery, who was seated across the desk from Whittington, then back at Lisa. "I'll pass your thank-you along to him later," he replied. "But with the way Whittington's feeling right now, inside that office is the last place in San Angelo you want to be." He glanced around. "Where's your rig? I'll walk you to it, and you can get on home."

"What? No escort this evening?" Lisa asked in a half-joking tone.

It was the portion of her voice that wasn't joking that caught Cody's attention. Though he hadn't considered riding out to the Kingston ranch until that moment, now he couldn't think of anything that sounded better. Holding up a finger telling her to wait a moment, he poked his head back into the office and announced his intentions to Vickery, then turned to Lisa. In an official-sounding voice he announced, "Ma'am, you are now under the escort of the Texas Rangers, Company C of the Frontier Battalion."

Playing along, Lisa coyly batted her eyelashes as Cody untied his gelding and strolled with her to her buggy, tied a block down the street. "Then I'm in your capable hands, Mr. Cody." In the next instant the playfulness vanished. "Why was the sheriff so riled, anyway?"

Cody swung into the saddle while Lisa climbed into the rig and backed her horse into the street. "He was ambushed by the mayor and town council today."

"Oh?"

"Seems the mayor gave him an invite to lunch. When Whittington showed up, he found the whole council lying in wait for him. Apparently they don't think the sheriff is doing all that he can over these murders. The fact that the Rangers haven't had any better success didn't change the way they feel," he added heatedly. "They've given the sheriff a week to have the killer behind bars or hand in his resignation. They don't have the slightest idea what kind of maniac we're dealing with."

Cody suddenly realized how much his words must have stung Lisa, whose wound from her father's death was still all too fresh. "I'm sorry. I didn't mean to sound off about something that's so painful for you."

"I understand. But I don't think you're aware of what the mayor and council are dealing with," Lisa said. "The whole town's on edge. Everyone knows about the killings. They've heard the horrible details. They know how the killer cuts his victims, then takes the ears. And they're scared, Cody. All the merchants I dealt with today won't let their wives out on the streets alone, even in broad daylight. San Angelo isn't the safest town in Texas to begin with, but this . . . this is something hard for the mind to grasp."

Cody was taken aback. He'd been so wrapped up in the daily routine of the investigation that he'd paid no attention to the town's mood. Of course the killings would prey on the minds of San Angelo's residents. The murders refused to leave his *own* thoughts.

"Will a week be enough time?" Lisa asked. "I mean, will it be enough once Whittington puts your plan into effect?"

"I don't know," Cody admitted, shaking his head. "The killer's been striking every other night. If we can get the men into place by tomorrow night like the sheriff wants, and if luck is riding on our shoulders, then we might get our man."

"*Tomorrow* night?" Lisa turned to him, worry lining her face. "If the killer strikes every other night, that means he'll kill again tonight."

"I've thought of that," the Ranger answered. "I've also thought about last night. He was out last night. That doesn't fit his pattern."

"Do you think he's starting to move every night?"

"I'm not certain what to think," Cody said as he scanned the dusk-cloaked terrain. "But our man has a strong taste for killing, and the only way he'll stop is for us to stop him."

Lisa was silent for the rest of the ride to her ranch. It wasn't until her house was in sight that she looked at the Ranger riding beside her. "When you offered to escort me home, I thought that the least I could do would be to cook you supper. Especially after last night. But, frankly, I don't feel up to cooking. Though I can offer you some leftover fried chicken and some cornbread. And fresh coffee."

"Chicken and cornbread sounds just fine," Cody assured her. He pointed to a porch swing. "Specially if we could eat there and enjoy the evening breeze."

Lisa smiled her approval. "We'll make it a front-porch picnic. I'll get the food if you'll take this rig back to the barn and unharness Reb. There's grain and water already waiting in his stall."

"Lady, you've got yourself a deal."

By the time the Ranger returned from the barn, Lisa had a platter heaped with chicken and cornbread and two glasses of lemonade sitting on a low table beside the porch swing.

"I decided that lemonade seemed more appropriate for a picnic than coffee," she explained.

Cody had no complaints about the beverage or the food or the gentle rhythm of the swing or the coolness of the night breeze. But more than all that, he had no complaints about being with Lisa Kingston. The sound of a voice that didn't belong to Vickery or Whittington or one of the seven suspects they continually questioned was a welcome diversion from the routine of almost a week in San Angelo. He felt comfortable with the young woman, and their unforced conversation flowed easily, whether the subject was the ranch she now intended to run herself or Cody's service in the Rangers or life on the frontier in general. He lost track of time until he noticed the low-riding moon moving toward the western horizon.

"It's getting late," he said, regretting having to draw the pleasant evening to a close. "I should be heading back to town."

For a response Lisa turned and leaned toward Cody. Her lips pressed against his, lingering there beyond the point of a simple good-night kiss. When she shifted away, it was with a soft sigh. "I've been wanting to do that again since last night."

"The same thought passed through my mind a few dozen times today." Cody eased her back to him.

This time their kiss had no hint of parting. When their lips separated, it was only for Cody's mouth to glide down the smooth arch of her neck.

If asked how they'd moved from porch swing to bedroom, Cody would've been hard-pressed to give details, but a trail of shed clothing through the house marked the progress of their mounting desire. The Ranger did feel a twinge of conscience when an image of Hope Baxter flitted unbidden and uncomfortably through his brain, but the sight of Lisa stretched atop a luxuriously large feather bed, the moonlight bathing her nakedness as she lifted her arms to him, washed away any hesitation. Cody needed no further invitation or inducement. He went to her.

CHAPTER
‖‖‖‖‖‖‖‖‖‖‖‖‖‖‖‖‖‖‖‖‖ **12** ‖‖‖‖‖‖‖‖‖‖‖‖‖‖‖‖‖‖‖‖

Straddling the girl's body, the killer reached under his coat and withdrew the blue Army blouse. With the point of his knife he poked a small hole in the sleeve, then used his finger to rip it down the length of the arm, making it appear that the shirt had been torn in a struggle. Leaning over, he dipped the front of the shirt in the warm blood that still flowed from the now-lifeless form.

Standing up, he looked at his handiwork and chuckled softly. How easy it was! No one could stop someone as superior as he—especially the two bungling Texas Rangers, whom he'd managed to evade with such ease. To think that he had once thought them so clever and had been so fearful of them.

He knew better now.

He'd use the shirt to make total fools of the Rangers and Whittington by putting it where they would easily find it in the morning, yet it would look like they'd stumbled onto it by accident. With such evidence in their hands, they'd have but one course to take, one man to arrest. Tonight he would set the wheels in motion, then stand back and watch Cody, Vickery, and Whittington lead an innocent man to the gallows.

"What the hell?" Sheriff Whittington's voice unexpectedly came from the entrance to the narrow alley. "Who's in there? Come on out! Do you hear me? Come on out now!"

The killer didn't hesitate—or do as the sheriff commanded. Pivoting, he darted for the other end of the alley.

Behind him he heard the lawman move forward with cautious steps. Then he heard a horrified groan. Whittington had found the body.

"You bastard!" Whittington screamed. "Stop, you son of a bitch, or I'll shoot!"

The killer didn't stop. He reached the end of the alley and turned left, running behind the shops and stores that lined San Angelo's main street. The darkness effectively shielded him, so though he heard the lawman fire behind him, he knew Whittington was firing blindly and the bullets wouldn't find their target. Still clutching the bloody blouse, the killer ran toward Fort Concho and the river.

Cody abruptly reined in the brown gelding as he entered the heart of San Angelo. The warm pleasure he was still feeling from his interlude with Lisa Kingston evaporated immediately, replaced by dread. Some twenty men were gathered in front of the jail. They didn't appear to have come on a social visit.

Clucking the gelding forward, the Ranger halted at a hitchrack a dozen yards up the block from the jail, where he dismounted and tethered the horse. He walked quickly to the jail and pushed his way through the crowd of men to find Deputy Todman standing outside the door, a shotgun in hand.

"What's going on?" Cody asked the deputy.

Todman grinned. "While you was out havin' yourself a moonlight ride with Miss Kingston, the sheriff's done gone and caught himself a killer. Got him locked up safe and sound inside. Go on in and take a look for yourself. Seems like the sheriff didn't need no Texas Rangers to do his job for him after all."

Cody ignored Todman's sneering tone and stepped into the office.

"No, Captain, I think it's you who doesn't understand," Sheriff Whittington was saying to Captain Harrington and four soldiers from Fort Concho. "I ain't about to turn Lieutenant Harper over to you and your darkie soldiers. The way I read the law, four killin's took place in my town, which puts the murderin' bastard under my jurisdiction. And that's where he'll stay till we can get us a circuit judge."

Four killings? Lieutenant Harper? Cody thought with astonishment. Apparently a lot had happened during the few hours he'd spent with Lisa.

"I was afraid it would come to this, Sheriff," Harrington said. His right hand slipped to his sidearm. "But the major gave me strict orders to return Lieutenant Harper to the fort's stockade, where he'll await military court-martial. And that's what I intend to do."

As Harrington started to slip his pistol from his holster, Cody leapt forward, and his left hand closed around the officer's wrist, clamping down. "I wouldn't do that, Captain."

Unable to free his right hand, Harrington struck out with his left. Cody's own left arm shot up, and he blocked the roundhouse punch intended for his head with his forearm. But his elbow didn't stop. It continued upward to connect solidly with the officer's chin, and Harrington collapsed to his knees. Cody now held the officer's pistol in his right hand, and he cocked it and swung it to cover the four soldiers who moved in to help their commander.

"So far all we've got is one sore jaw. There's no need for anyone going and getting himself seriously hurt," Cody said, aiming the weapon directly between the eyes of the nearest soldier.

The four froze, glanced at Harrington, then backed away, apparently deciding the captain wasn't worth dying for.

"That's better." Cody's heart pounded like a bass drum. He wasn't certain what he'd stepped into, but he was right in the middle of it, and he didn't like it.

"I think I'd better take those rifles," Captain Vickery said. He stepped forward and took the rifles from the soldiers. "I'll see that these are returned to the fort in the mornin'. But for now, lettin' you keep 'em might prove too big a temptation."

Whittington nudged Harrington with the toe of a boot. "Captain, I think you and your men better get on out of here before I decide to toss the lot of you in a cell for the night. I don't appreciate a man tryin' to throw down on me."

The Army captain managed to stand, though he swayed uneasily for a few seconds. His eyes narrowing in anger, he warned the sheriff, "This isn't the last you'll be hearing from me. Harper's an officer; he belongs to the Army."

"That well may be," Vickery spoke up, "but it's a decision to be made by a judge's rulin', not by a gun. Best run on back to the fort like the sheriff said, 'cause if he don't toss your backside in jail in the next minute for attempted assault, I will."

For a moment Cody thought Harrington was going to be foolish enough to argue. Instead, he turned to his men and told them, "We'll return to the fort."

With that he marched the soldiers out of the office and into the night.

Letting his breath out slowly, Cody lowered the pistol's hammer and placed the six-gun on Whittington's desk. "Anyone mind telling me what's going on?"

"Our killer struck again tonight," Whittington replied, his face somber. "A girl by the name of Sarah Beth Laird. Just turned seventeen, she had. She was to be married next month."

"The sheriff heard noise in an alley near the seamstress shop where the girl had been gettin' a fittin' for her weddin' dress," Vickery added, picking up the story. "When he went to take a look, the killer ran."

Whittington recounted firing two shots as he chased the man through dark alleys toward the Concho River. "I wasn't close enough to get a good look at him. Fact was, I was afraid he was goin' to get away from me. I'm not as young as I used to be, and I was never built for runnin'. Down near Brandon's Tannery, he made a mistake. I saw him toss somethin' toward the scrap barrels behind the tannery."

Opening the bottom drawer of his desk, the lawman pulled out a bloodstained Army blouse. Cody examined the torn shirt and found Harper's name neatly stitched into the collar.

"From the looks of it, the girl put up a fight," Vickery said as Cody handed the blouse back to the sheriff. "The shirt's pretty damnin' by itself, but Sheriff Whittington found more."

Cody looked back at the sheriff, who nodded. "When I stopped to see what the killer had tossed, I lost him. But once I got a gander at the Army blouse I knew exactly where to head. And what with the name so conveniently sewn into the shirt for launderin' purposes, I didn't even have to do any investigatin'. Then it turned out I didn't even have to go all the way to the fort. I found Harper down by the river, naked as a jaybird and standin' in the water, hurryin' to wash away the blood. Had his clothes laid out on the bank as neat as you please, includin' a fresh blouse."

Cody shoved back his hat and said, "Looks like you caught him dead to rights, Sheriff. Mighty fine piece of work. Kinda surprising that he was wearing his uniform tonight, though," he added, uncertainty niggling at the back of his mind. "Last night the man Cap'n Vickery and I saw was dressed all in black."

"What about his skin?" Whittington asked. "Was *it* black?"

"Couldn't tell. I was too far away, and he kept to the shadows."

"I reckon it don't matter what you saw last night." Whittington pointed to the desk drawer. "This shirt's all I need. And it's all a jury'll need to get Harper an appointment with a hangman."

"I guess you're right," Cody said. He couldn't dispute the evidence. They'd worked with the hope that eventually the killer would make a mistake. It seemed he'd made more than one that night. For a man who'd been so careful, his actions that night didn't seem to fit. "He must've panicked."

"Huh?" Vickery asked, staring at his colleague. "Panicked, you say?"

Cody shrugged. "Just thinking aloud. He's been so damned careful up until tonight. It almost seems out of character for him to make so many mistakes."

"He got cocky," Whittington said. The sheriff's tone and stance were defensive. "He made one mistake, and it led to another and another and another. That's what we were hopin' would happen, wasn't it?"

"Exactly what we wanted," Cody agreed. "You caught him red-handed. A jury will see that."

Whittington nodded with finality. "Damned right they will. That son of a bitch is gonna leave this life with his neck stretched two or three inches longer than it is now."

The sheriff's certainty didn't quiet the niggling doubt in Cody's mind. He needed to hear Harper's story. "Mind if I take a look at your prisoner?"

Whittington waved an arm toward the door leading to the cells. "Gawk at the bastard all you want."

As Cody strode toward the cellblock door, Vickery said to the local lawman, "Reckon Cody and I can head back to Del Rio come tomorrow."

"Actually, I'd like for you two to stay on awhile longer, Captain," Whittington replied. "I'm goin' to get a wire off to Austin tonight and see about gettin' a judge in here as soon as possible. You two are prime witnesses." He paused a moment, then added, "And I reckon I wouldn't mind havin' two extra hands around in case of trouble. This town ain't gonna want to wait for a judge to make Harper's hangin' all nice and legal."

"Very well. Cody and I will stay on as long as we're needed," Vickery replied.

Cody entered the cellblock and closed the door behind him. He didn't object to laying over in San Angelo a little longer. Lisa Kingston had suddenly made the town a nice place to be.

He walked down the aisle to Harper's cell.

"You come to stare at the nigger killer, Ranger?" the lieutenant asked. His voice was steeped in bitterness as he looked up from the cot he sat on.

Cody stepped to the bars. "I came to hear your side of what happened tonight."

Harper sat silently as though considering whether or not to answer; finally he spoke. "I haven't killed anyone. As I told Sheriff Whittington, the only one of those murdered whom I knew was Rosa Aguilar. She took in laundry, and I had taken my dirty clothing to her earlier this week to be washed. Several officers recommended her. I suspect that's where your killer got my shirt."

Cody wondered if maybe washing wasn't all that had been recommended about the young prostitute. "And you claim you never heard of the others?"

"Heard of, yes. When you and Captain Vickery and Sheriff Whittington mentioned them," the lieutenant replied.

That Harper wasn't acquainted with those killed in San Angelo was inconsequential, as far as Cody was concerned. He had assumed from the beginning that the butcher hadn't known any of his victims.

"Why were you in the river tonight?" Cody asked.

"I was bathing."

"Bathing?"

"Surely you've heard of bathing, Ranger. It's when a man washes himself." Harper's usual arrogance had returned. "I know *some* people do it around here. They sell baths at barbershops—but not to me. My skin's black, you see. That leaves me having to bathe in the river, which I do after sunset."

"Is there anyone at the fort who can confirm your bathing habits?" Cody asked. "Especially tonight?"

"I didn't announce my intentions to anyone. I went for a walk, and while I was by the river, I decided to bathe. It's hot tonight. The water looked cool."

"Another walk?" Cody recalled Harper had been out for a walk the night he supposedly discovered Calvin Kingston's body. "You certainly seem to be stretching your legs a lot."

"It's the heat, Ranger. I'm from northern New York. By October there's usually frost on the ground, if not snow. I'm not used to this Texas heat. I've had trouble sleeping ever since I crossed the Red River. I walk every night, sometimes for hours."

"And you walk alone?"

Harper nodded. "The heat doesn't seem to bother anyone else. I usually walk by the river. It's cooler there."

"Anyone ever happen to see you?" Cody pressed.

"The guards see me come and go," Harper answered, "but that's about it. The river's quiet at night. That's why I like it."

Cody shook his head. "For a man about to have his neck stuck in a noose, you don't have much of a story, Lieutenant."

Harper glared at the Ranger. "It's the truth, so it's the only story I have. And even if I had a hundred witnesses, it wouldn't matter," he said heatedly. "The sheriff's got my blouse, and he's got the nigger who goes in it. That's all that matters to him or anyone else."

Cody stared at the young officer, who abruptly stretched out on the cot and closed his eyes, effectively dismissing his visitor. Turning from the cell, Cody headed back to the office, slowly shaking his head. He'd seen a thousand hardcases put behind bars. They all reacted differently when caught. Some pleaded innocence; others spat in the face of their captors. Harper's cool arrogance wasn't out of the ordinary.

"Well?" Whittington asked when Cody reentered the office. "What do you think?"

"I think you caught our man," Cody replied. The niggling doubt at the back of his mind was still there, but it didn't squirm as much as it had before he'd seen Harper. "You did a fine job, Sheriff. I guess we can all rest easy now."

CHAPTER
13

N igger lover!" a voice called out. "You ought to string up the black bastard and quit wastin' time!"

Cody released Lisa Kingston's arm and spun around. At least thirty people were in his immediate vicinity on the street, either passing by or peering into shop windows. None of them looked at the Ranger; all went about their business as though they'd heard nothing.

Lisa took Cody's arm again and whispered, "Let it go. It's just someone blowing off steam. The whole town is tied in knots."

Cody continued on toward the sheriff's office. "What worries me is that it's not steam being vented, but some combustible gas."

Lisa's green eyes shifted from left to right, surveying the town. "Things are starting to feel rather nasty, aren't they?"

"Nastier by the minute," Cody replied. They reached the sheriff's office, and he stopped. Gesturing inside, he remarked, "It's been three days since Harper was locked up in there—three days and not another killing. Folks are thinking that we've obviously got the right man behind bars, so maybe there's no need to wait for the circuit judge."

"What about you?" Lisa asked, her gaze fixed on the Ranger's face. "Do you still have some doubts about Harper?"

"No more than I had to begin with."

"You mean Harper being dressed in his uniform rather than in black?"

"And the lack of blood on his breeches—not even the tiniest spatter—though the blouse Whittington saw him throw away was covered with blood. Plus the fact we didn't find a black suit among his things."

"But like you just said, it's been three days since Harper was arrested, and there haven't been any more killings."

Cody pushed open the door, replying, "That more than anything says we've got the right man locked up. I just wish the judge could get here sooner. This town feels like a powder keg about to explode."

"It'll get worse before it gets better," Whittington said, seated behind his desk. He nodded toward Captain Vickery, who sat across from him. "We just heard the mayor's called a town meetin' for tonight. Want to place bets on what the main topic of discussion'll be?"

"Harper," Cody replied.

"You hit the nail on the head," Whittington said. "Oh, the official reason might be raisin' funds for a larger schoolhouse, but you can bet a year's pay that Harper'll be all that's talked about."

"Nastier and nastier," Cody mumbled under his breath.

"Most folks hereabouts think it'd save the town a lot of money if the lieutenant was just strung up from the nearest tree and to hell with the judge and a trial," Whittington said. "Not that I blame 'em none. If I wasn't wearin' a badge, I'd probably side with 'em."

Vickery looked up at Cody. "The sheriff's expectin' trouble after the town meetin' breaks up tonight. If you and Miss Kingston have any plans, you'd best postpone 'em."

Cody frowned. A town with lynching on its mind was not a pretty sight. It was even less attractive to have to face head on. "Any men in town we can get to stand against a mob, if one forms?"

Whittington shook his head. "Ain't a man in town who's gonna put his life on the line for Harper."

"Five against the rest of the town." Cody shoved back his hat. "Those aren't the kind of odds a man likes to have backing his hand."

"It might be only three makin' a stand," Whittington said. "Welch and Todman are good men when it comes to keepin' this town quiet, but I wouldn't count on 'em to stand by us tonight. I don't think either man would consider it smart to risk takin' a slug to stop Harper from gettin' his neck stretched."

Cody stroked his mustache. "I reckon one of us had best attend this town meeting tonight and try to keep a lid on things."

The killer left the town hall amid angry citizens pushing onto the street. He struggled to keep a smug smile off his face. The bloodied shirt had completely thrown the sheriff and the Rangers off his trail. He had pulled the wool over their eyes, making them, like the rest of the town, blind to the truth.

He moved off, away from those milling together in the middle of the street, their anger mounting with each passing second. He was safe; that was what mattered. All he had to do was bide his time until Harper was hanged and San Angelo was again quiet. Soon—a month from now, he'd decided—he'd be moving on, going all the way to California. He'd have to control his hunger until he left San Angelo.

Except for one time, he thought with a pleased smile. The night after Harper's hanging he'd kill again so that Whittington and the Rangers would know their mistake— know the feel of innocent blood on their hands. He would see to that.

The thought of that moment of triumph set his hunger stirring. *No!* He shoved the thought from his mind. He deliberately kept his hand away from the pocket that held the sheathed skinning knife. Tonight he was safe, and he intended to maintain that safety.

Buttoning his coat against the cool night air, the temperature finally feeling like October, he quickened his stride. He had set aside tonight for fondling his trophies, still hidden in the Masons' woodshed. Admiring his prizes would give him enough pleasure to hold him until he could kill again.

He accelerated his pace even more.

Across the street from the Mason house he stopped in the deep shadow of a mesquite tree, where he looked up and down the street several times to make certain he wouldn't be seen. Tonight was no time to be careless.

He was about to head across the street when the back door of the Mason house opened, and Clara Mason, a lantern in hand, came out and started across the lawn toward the woodshed. The killer's temples began pounding. *The damnable woman!* his brain screamed. She reached the shed, opened the door, and went inside.

His fear mounting, he crept closer, scurrying into the dark shadow of a large shrub growing near the back door. He watched as Clara set down the lantern and picked up several lengths of wood. The killer suddenly realized he had been lulled by the unseasonal warmth into ignoring the danger of using the woodpile as a hiding place for his trophies. Now it was too late. Clara picked up another log, then stopped and peered into the stack of firewood. Putting down the wood, she picked up the lantern and held it over the woodpile, then reached in and pulled out the pouch of oiled leather. Clara had found his secret place!

She untied the pouch's drawstrings and emptied the contents onto the stack of firewood.

A shriek tore from her throat, and she tossed the pouch away in horror, scattering the ears in the process, then ran into the house. The killer cringed. Her scream seemed to hang on the night air like a clarion call.

This changed everything. It meant that he wouldn't be leaving San Angelo in a month. He'd be leaving that very night.

Captain Vickery raced into the sheriff's office and slammed the door, sweat dotting his brow despite the cool evening. He looked from Cody to Lisa to Whittington and shook his head slowly.

"I just came from the hotel, and I got to tell you, it's gettin' real ugly out there. One heck of an angry mob is formin' up the street, and I don't think there's much chance of them breakin' up and goin' home peaceably. That Sonny Laird's incitin' 'em. He wants Harper real bad for what he did to his daughter."

Sheriff Whittington pushed from his desk and stood up. "Maybe I can go talk some sense into 'em—specially Sonny."

He walked over and took a double-barreled shotgun down from a wall rack, then turned for the door, but Vickery placed a hand on his shoulder. "I don't think one man'll be able to talk any sense into that throng. The only thing he might accomplish is gettin' himself hurt."

Anguish mixed with desperation crossed the sheriff's face. "That bad?"

"That bad," Vickery confirmed with a nod. "They're gearin' up for a confrontation, no matter what. The best we can do is wait right here and meet 'em when they come to us. This ain't no time to split up."

Whittington stared out the window for a moment, then asked, "You happen to see Welch or Todman?"

"I did. Your deputies are standin' outside a saloon with beers in their hands. They haven't joined in with the rest, but they're not doin' anythin' to stop 'em. I think they've made their decision."

The sheriff reached for the badge pinned to his leather vest, his fingers toying with the star as though he considered yanking it off. Finally his hand dropped back to his side. "They probably made a damned sight smarter move than any of us. The folks out there aren't gonna be thinkin' straight when they come down here. They won't give a damn about us. All they'll want is Harper."

"It's our job to stop 'em from gettin' him," Vickery said. "And our job is what these people—and all the people of Texas—pay us to do."

Whittington snorted. "Then we don't get paid nearly enough. Fact is, there ain't enough money to make a man do what we have to do," he said as he passed the shotgun to Vickery. "You'll be needin' this. A scattergun's best when it comes to workin' in close."

Cody agreed with the sheriff: It wasn't money that gathered them in the office; it was a basic belief that a world ruled by law was far better than one ruled by chaos. Sometimes a man had to stand up for that belief, even if it might cost him his life. Tonight was one of those times. They sure as hell didn't like it, but they accepted what had to be done.

One person in the office, though, had no business there. Cody turned to Lisa and told her, "I think it's time you were going. It'll turn rough before too long. No need for you to get hurt."

But for the first time in days the Ranger saw the steel return to Lisa's spine. Ignoring Cody's suggestion, she turned to Whittington and said, "Sheriff, I can handle a shotgun. I'll take one and a box of shells."

The lawman willingly complied with her request.

As the young woman broke open the scattergun Whittington handed her and dropped two shells into the barrels, Cody stepped in front of her. "You don't know what you're getting yourself into," he said. "That's a lynch mob forming outside. You heard the sheriff: They'll be after one thing, and they won't give a damn about anyone who gets in their way."

Lisa snapped the shotgun together and hefted it to her shoulder, getting a feel for the weapon. Satisfied, she lowered it. "Look, Cody, my father was murdered by Harper. I want him to get what's coming to him more than anyone outside, with the exception of Sonny Laird. But I want him to stand trial and climb a gallows stairs. Everything legal. I don't want any doubts surrounding his hanging. I won't hesitate using this if someone tries to take that away from me."

"You sure of that, young lady?" Vickery asked, eyeing her closely.

"As sure as I am of wanting to see my father's killer hanged," Lisa answered firmly.

Vickery hesitated. He glanced at Whittington, who nodded. "Then I reckon we can use all the help we can get. I don't think you should be outside, but we can use someone inside, guardin' this door when the time comes."

Lisa walked to the desk and dragged a chair from beside it, positioning it halfway between the front door and the door to the cells. Sitting down, she pointed to the front door. "I'll shoot the first man who comes through there who isn't supposed to. The second, too. And if there's time to reload, the third and fourth."

Vickery smiled in obvious admiration. "Young lady, I do believe that's exactly what you'll do."

"It is," Lisa said coolly.

Cody didn't like Lisa placing herself in harm's way, but in their short time together he'd learned that once her mind was made up, nothing in heaven or on earth would change it. He silently cursed the very spirit that had first attracted him to the young woman—while admitting the same admiration the captain felt.

" 'Pears like the time for talkin's run out," the sheriff said. He closed the wooden shutter to the window he stood beside, then pointed to the other window, which Cody shuttered. "They're comin' down the street, and it ain't a tea social they've got on their minds."

Vickery glanced at Cody and the sheriff. "I say we meet 'em face to face outside. If they get a good gander at these scatterguns, it might give 'em pause to think."

Whittington crossed to the front door, then looked back at Lisa in her chair. "Lock and bar the door once we're outside," he instructed. "If anybody 'cept one of us tries to come through, do what you have to."

Lisa nodded, and Whittington stepped outside, Vickery at his heels. Cody paused long enough to plant a hasty kiss on Lisa's lips. "Miss Kingston, you're one hell of a woman."

Despite the fear that paled her face she smiled. "I know that. I was wondering when you would."

After another quick kiss Cody joined his fellow lawmen outside, making sure Lisa closed the door, then locked and barred it behind him. His attention then focused on the fifty men who marched down the middle of the street straight for the jail.

"They don't look liquored up that much," Vickery remarked.

Whittington nodded. "That might work in our favor. Clear heads are easier to talk sense into."

Reason and sense had little to do with any lynch mob he'd ever seen, Cody thought. He thumbed back the twin hammers of his shotgun.

"Earl," a voice called from the middle of the mob, "you and them Rangers step aside. We ain't out to hurt any of you."

The mob of men parted, and Sonny Laird stepped forward. The father of the murdered seventeen-year-old held a rope in his hands. A hangman's noose was tied in one end.

"Sonny, you know very well I can't do that," Whittington said, shifting his weight from one leg to the other, an action that brought the barrels of his scattergun around to point directly at the man. "You and the other good folks of San Angelo hired me to stop things like this from happenin'."

"We hired you to catch bastards that go around killin' folks the way that black son of a bitch killed my Sarah Beth," Laird responded. "You done your job, Earl. Now, you and them Rangers stand aside and let us do ours. Ain't nobody in town gonna think less of you if you do."

Whittington shouldered the double-barreled shotgun, holding it steadily on Laird. "Reckon it ain't a matter of what people think of me, Sonny. It's a matter of doin' what I was hired to do. Right now, that's protectin' my prisoner until a judge and jury have a go at him."

Cody constantly scanned the crowd. With two barrels staring down his throat, Sonny Laird wasn't likely to be the first to make a move. But any one of the other fifty or so men might suddenly decide to draw a pistol and attempt to eliminate the lawmen blocking the way to the jail.

"You ain't goin' to pull them triggers, Earl," someone shouted from the back of the crowd. "You know all of us. Hell, are you goin' to kill friends just to protect some murderin' nigger?"

The exploding blast of a shotgun answered before the sheriff could reply. A shocked rumble ran through the mob as the men backstepped a few paces.

Vickery lowered the scattergun that he'd fired above the men's heads and took a step forward. "Maybe you're right about the sheriff here not wantin' to open up on friends and neighbors. But I don't know a soul here, so that doesn't go for me. Why doesn't the man doin' all the talkin' back yonder step forward and see if I mean business or not?"

Dozens of heads turned to the rear of the mob, but the owner of the voice declined the captain's invitation.

"Why don't ya'll go home to your families and let the law take care of this?" Whittington said while Vickery broke open his shotgun and replaced the spent shell.

Sonny Laird, who had stood his ground, spoke again. "We can't do that, Earl. There's too big a chance the Army will bring in a high-powered lawyer to get Harper off. We know what he done. And we're gonna make sure he pays for it."

"Then I reckon you'll be joinin' your Sarah Beth before the night's out." Whittington's shotgun left no doubt as to the meaning of his threat. To make certain of that he added, "If any of you takes a step forward, Sonny'll be the first to die."

"And then we'll just open up," Vickery put in. "There's no way we'll get all of you, but we'll get quite a few 'fore you take us. You boys up front might consider changin' position with those back yonder."

Again heads turned toward the rear, but no man made a move. Cody knew Vickery wasn't bluffing. He hoped the men standing before them knew it, too.

Sonny Laird glared defiantly at Sheriff Whittington. "Earl, I reckon you're gonna have to do what you have to do. But I have a score to settle with the man you got locked inside. After what he did to my little Sarah Beth, I can't turn and walk away."

The door to the office suddenly swung open; Lisa stepped outside, shotgun cocked and ready. She walked forward until she stood beside Cody and Vickery, then eyed Laird. "What about my father's murder? Don't you think I want to see Harper get what he deserves? Of course I do. But I don't want it this way. Lynching the man would be no good. It would be no different from what he did to our loved ones."

At Lisa's appearance uncertainty shadowed several faces at the forefront of the crowd. Had Sonny Laird not been at their lead, Cody suspected many would have turned and retreated to their homes. But Laird was their leader. When he continued to stand his ground, the others loyally stayed with him.

"Miss Lisa, me and your daddy were friends for most of our lives," Laird answered. "He'd understand what I have to do. Why don't you just step aside and let me do it?"

Cody saw Lisa's hands tremble. In a daring move she'd played her high card, hoping her appearance would shame the men. It hadn't. Now she had no idea how to continue.

"Slip back inside and lock the door," Cody whispered.

Lisa's gaze darted to him, and she nodded in compliance. She then looked back at Laird. "Mr. Laird, I can't do what you ask. I'm going back inside, and I promise I'll open up on the first man coming through the door who doesn't belong there."

She looked from side to side while she backstepped toward the doorway. She was a single step from the threshold when she stopped and peered to her left. "Reverend Mason?"

Cody looked in the same direction. The preacher, astride a black mount, reined in at the fringe of the mob. Mason just sat there unmoving, staring at the crowd as though surprised to find all those men blocking the street.

"Reverend, this ain't no place for a man of God," Sonny Laird called out. "Turn that horse around and go on back to your home."

Mason's eyes suddenly grew wide, like a man startled from sleep. "You are wrong, Sonny Laird. This is exactly where I'm supposed to be." He nudged his heels against the horse's side and reined the horse closer to the jail. "I am supposed to help guide men along the path of righteousness and keep their feet from straying into the canyons of damnation. At this moment that's exactly where every one of you men are headed."

"Reverend Mason," someone called from the crowd, "this ain't Sunday mornin', you ain't standin' in the pulpit, and we ain't here to listen to a sermon."

"It would be a prettier sight to my eyes if all you men were seated in pews before my pulpit rather than here, Tate

Boyd," Mason answered, identifying the man as he halted his mount beside the jail and dismounted. "It would be far easier under those circumstances to explain to your little Rebecca what you were doing—and why. How old is she now, Tate? Six?"

"Turned six last week," the man replied.

"How are you going to explain to her you killed a man tonight, Tate?" Mason asked, stepping beside Sheriff Whittington. "Or how am I going to tell her that her daddy was killed trying to lynch a man?"

Searching the faces in the mob, Cody found the man the preacher addressed. His expression was one of confusion as he lowered a rifle he held.

"And you, Melvin Elrod, it won't be any easier for me to explain to your three children what's going to happen here." Mason pointed to a man near the front of the mob, then pivoted to the side to jab a finger at another. "Reese Abshire, you and Mary just had your first. What are you going to tell your son when he gets old enough to ask if you were here this night? And Keith Crider, what about your Sam and Amy? Will your children's breasts swell with pride to learn their pa helped lynch a man?"

One by one, Mason called out the names of those who stood ready to drag a man from a cell and hang him from the nearest tree. Here and there Cody saw men begin to fall back and turn away as the preacher threw the shame of what they were doing into their faces. What began as one man quietly drifting away quickly grew to three and four at a time, then five and six, as Mason continued his roll call of would-be vigilantes.

"Sonny Laird, your sorrow is great. I don't pretend to understand how deep it has cut into you," Mason said as he turned to Laird when only twenty or so men remained behind him. "I do know your wife and your two sons. What possible good will you be to them dead? And how will killing a man return your Sarah Beth to you? Terrible wrongs have been committed in this town. Do you really want to add to that number?"

Laird stared wordlessly at the preacher for a protracted moment; then he looked down at his feet. Without a word he turned and walked away. The remaining men, their heads hanging, followed their leader.

Cody slowly exhaled, and he realized he'd been holding his breath. It was over. Reverend Mason's words had achieved what loaded shotguns could not.

"Reverend, after tonight you can bet I'll be sittin' in the front row of your church to see what you're like in the pulpit!" Vickery said, reaching out and clapping the preacher's shoulder. "If you can move men like that, you must bring 'em to the Lamb in droves!"

Mason sighed. "If that were true, this wouldn't have happened tonight."

Cody turned to look for Lisa. He found that she had returned to the office and was sitting slumped in her chair with the shotgun on the floor beside her. Feeling the Ranger's gaze, she managed a smile and said, "I'm all right. I just feel drained."

Cody smiled back. "That makes two of us."

Whittington thanked the preacher for his aid, then said, "I think we can breathe easy, but it'd be best if we checked the town. If some of those men decided to have themselves a few drinks rather than goin' on to their homes, they might just convince themselves to try for Harper again."

"Good idea," Vickery concurred. "You guard the jail, and me and Cody'll make the rounds."

Cody started after the captain, then stopped and said to Whittington, "There's no need for Lisa to stay. She's done more than enough tonight. I'd feel better if she was safe in her own house." Cody shifted his gaze to the preacher. "I'd feel even better if there was someone to ride home with her. One of these men might not like what she did tonight and decide to try something."

Reverend Mason nodded solemnly. "I understand. I'll be happy to see that Miss Kingston arrives safely at her ranch."

"Thanks, Reverend. I'm much obliged."

With that, Cody joined Vickery for their rounds. The two men walked on opposite sides of the street toward the saloons and cathouses of San Angelo. Ten minutes passed quietly before they turned back toward the jail, this time walking down the middle of the street together. Reaching a corner a block from the sheriff's office, they stopped and eyed the street intersecting the main avenue.

"There's a few cantinas up yonder," Vickery said, nodding toward three well-lit saloons to the left. "We might as well check 'em out."

Cody agreed, then hefted the shotgun he still carried. "This is beginning to feel like dead weight. I think I'll run it back to the sheriff."

"Take mine with you," Vickery said, handing his shotgun to his fellow Ranger. "Never felt comfortable with a scattergun. Too heavy and not much range."

Leaving the captain waiting for him at the corner, Cody strode in double time to the jail, where he knocked on the door and announced himself. It took but seconds for Whittington to lift the bar and unlock the door.

"Everything all right?" the sheriff asked as he opened the door to admit the Ranger.

"Looks quiet and peaceable. Just wanted to return these to you." Cody walked across the room and returned the shotguns to the wall rack.

"If you happen to run into Welch or Todman, tell 'em I'd like to talk with 'em," Whittington said. "Tell 'em they still got a job if they ain't too shamed by what they did."

Cody nodded. "I'll do that."

He started toward the open door and abruptly stopped. Lifting his head, he sniffed deeply, catching a faint smell of sweetness on the air. A tingle ran up his spine. He recognized the sweet odor. He'd smelled it the night the man in black had eluded Vickery and him—the night he had followed Lisa Kingston.

"It's jasmine," Whittington said with an amused chuckle. "The preacher came in for a few moments while Lisa collected herself, and he always smells a mite like a French whorehouse. It's on his clothes. His wife, Clara, uses enough jasmine perfume to fill an ocean, and she's always burning jasmine incense."

"Damn!" Icy dread suddenly flowed in Cody's veins. He now recalled where he'd first noticed the smell—in Jacob Mason's home. It had been so overpowering there that his mind hadn't connected the scent of jasmine with this coy sweetness.

"Harper isn't the killer! It's the preacher!" Cody declared. "Get Cap'n Vickery in here and have him smell this. He'll understand. I'm going after Mason. He's got Lisa!"

Cody didn't wait for a response. He ran from the office, mounted the brown gelding outside, and spurred south toward the Kingston ranch. Mason had fifteen or twenty minutes on him. He prayed that the gelding's long legs could make up that time.

CHAPTER
14

When Whittington came looking for Captain Vickery and filled him in on Cody's conclusion, the Ranger stared at the sheriff as if *he* were a madman. "You must've heard Cody wrong," he told the local lawman. "Either that or all of Cody's reasoning has deserted him. The Reverend Mason can't possibly be the guilty one. No man who'd put his life on the line the way he did tonight with that mob could be such a heinous slayer of innocents."

All the way back to the sheriff's office Vickery tried to convince himself that Cody was wrong about Mason—despite the fact that Cody's instincts were usually right. After all, Whittington had Harper's bloody blouse in a desk drawer. That was solid evidence. It was hard to deny.

But the sweetness he now smelled inside Whittington's office was also hard to deny—the same scent that'd been in the air the night the man in black had followed Lisa Kingston. Mason always wore black.

Vickery quickly mounted up and headed out of town after Cody. The way out of San Angelo took him past the Reverend Mason's house. The front door was ominously wide open, and lamps seemed to be burning in every lower room of the two-story house. That seemed unusual for this hour of night. The hairs on the back of his neck began to stand up. Maybe Mason had decided there was no need to take Lisa Kingston all the way to her ranch. Maybe he'd simply brought her back here.

But no, that wouldn't make sense. There was Clara Mason to consider.

Clara Mason . . .

Feeling a terrible sense of dread, the Ranger captain hauled back on the reins, pulling up his mount. He dismounted and tied the horse to a cast-iron hitching post outside the Mason house, then started up the front walk.

Whipping out the Paterson Colt from its holster, Vickery thumbed back the hammer as he stepped onto the porch. He crossed to the open doorway and peered inside.

His stomach roiled. Cody was right.

Clara Mason lay in the hallway. Blood was pooled around her naked, butchered body and was splattered over the floral wallpaper. Like all the other victims, the woman's ears had been severed from her head.

Fighting the violent churning of his stomach, Vickery stepped inside. As quickly as caution allowed, he searched each room of the house, but except for the dead woman, the Mason home was empty. He took a tablecloth from the dining room and covered Clara Mason's bloody remains and left the house, closing the door behind him. Nothing further could be done here, and Cody was riding straight for a hell-spawned demon. He was the one who needed help. He and Lisa Kingston.

Holstering the Colt, Vickery hurried back to his horse, remounted, and headed southward. He prayed that Cody and Lisa wouldn't find out firsthand what he himself had too closely almost learned.

Lisa came back from unconsciousness to a throbbing ache that filled her head. Moaning, she blinked her eyes open. Reverend Jacob Mason stood above her. A maniacal grin twisted his face.

"*No!*" Lisa groaned, remembering now.

The preacher had escorted her to the door. When she had reached for the lamp on the table, something hard had slammed into the back of her head. That was all she recalled.

Her eyes darted about as she took in her situation. She

lay on her back atop her bed. She was tied spread-eagle to the bedposts.

"Yes," Mason said, chuckling with fiendish glee. "The answer is yes."

Lisa instinctively twisted toward the shotgun that she had left against the wall beside the headboard. But rope bit into her wrists and ankles, preventing her from grabbing the weapon that was mere inches from her straining fingertips.

"So near, yet so far," Mason said. He glanced at the weapon and the open hand that sought to grasp it. "I hadn't intended to taunt you so. Truly I hadn't."

"Reverend Mason, you must not do this," Lisa pleaded. She tried to gather her wits, to quell the runaway beating of her heart.

"You are wrong, my dear. I'm afraid I must."

Mason's hand slipped into his coat pocket, withdrawing the skinning knife. Reaching for the lamp on the nightstand, he turned up the wick slightly, brightening the room. The light glinted on the curved steel blade.

He ran a finger along the knife's honed edge. He didn't seem to notice that it nicked the skin and brought blood oozing to the surface. "I hadn't planned it this way, you know. I was going to wait until they hanged Harper before I enjoyed myself again. I wanted to show Whittington and those Rangers what idiots they were by executing the wrong man. They would have blood on their hands, and I would be safe in California."

Mason stared at the wall above Lisa's head. His gaze was distant as though he were looking at something that only he could see. "But Clara changed all that. She discovered my secret."

Lisa gasped. "You killed your wife!"

"She was hardly a wife," Mason replied. His eyes were chillingly cold. "No more than the woman who called herself my mother was a wife. Deaf, both of them. Deaf to any pleas and desires."

"But why me?" Lisa asked desperately. "I've done nothing to you."

The preacher smiled. His smile was even more chilling

than his eyes. "Why? Because I have a hunger—or perhaps it's a thirst—that must be satisfied. And you will satisfy it very nicely, my dear." His gaze dropped to his knife. "Now it's time to quench my thirst."

"Reverend Mason, please! Listen to me!" Lisa strained against the ropes binding her wrists; the hemp only bit deeper into her flesh. "Reverend, you saved the life of a man tonight. You don't want to kill. I know you don't!"

He laughed a high-pitched, almost hysterical laugh, and it was clear that he was deranged. "I *was* brilliant, wasn't I? I so completely convinced Whittington and the Rangers of my rectitude. I so completely made utter fools of them."

Without warning his left hand reached out and clamped down on her neck, immobilizing her. His right hand then began wielding the knife, using it to slowly, carefully, slice away the front of her dress. Her undergarments came next. He cut through the white cotton fabrics, then peeled them back until she lay naked on the bed.

"Now, you are ready to satisfy me." He leaned forward, knife blade turned down.

"*No!*" Lisa screamed. She threw herself against the ropes, twisting and turning, bucking wildly to escape. "No, damn you, no!"

A hand grasped her right shoulder, fingers like steel clamping into her flesh. He pinned her to the bed with a single hand while he brought the knife down. Lightly it brushed her skin just beneath her collarbone. Tiny droplets of blood oozed from the hairline cut. Lisa whimpered piteously with the realization that she was going to die.

"Please!" she begged. "Please, don't. Please!"

A smile twisted his lips as he drew the blade across her flesh three more times, three lines parallel to the first.

"Oh, God!" she sobbed. Tears rolled down her cheeks as Mason made a quick series of horizontal lines, crosshatching the four original cuts. "Please, don't do this! They'll catch you. They'll know you did this!"

"It doesn't matter." Mason leaned back as though to admire his handiwork. "I want them to know."

He leaned forward again, knife blade raised and poised to cut deep, when suddenly he sat upright. He jerked his head toward the open bedroom door, anger darkening his face.

Hooves! She heard them, too! A horse was approaching the ranch house. She knew who the rider would be. "Cody!" she shrieked. "Cody, help me!"

Mason twisted back to her. Glaring at her, he slammed his fist into her chin. With a moan Lisa dropped into the blackness of unconsciousness.

A desperate cry, muffled by distance and the pounding of the gelding's hooves, reached Cody's ears. Then it was gone, cut off abruptly.

Lisa! The Ranger's heart doubled its wild racing. She was still alive. He refused to consider that the blade Jacob Mason wielded might be the reason that her call had been cut short. She still lived. She had to. He couldn't have come this close only to lose her. He couldn't!

He peered at the limestone ranch house. Light from the waning moon revealed that the front door stood wide open. A dim yellow glow came from within, no doubt a single lamp burning from some back room.

He suddenly blinked. Had the night played tricks on his eyes, or for a fleeting instant had a shadow moved through the light?

Repressing the urge to answer Lisa's cry, to reassure her that she would be all right, Cody yanked back hard on the reins. Dirt and stone sprayed the air as the gelding slid to a halt in front of the house.

Before the animal was fully stopped, Cody leapt from the saddle. He hit the ground in a dead run that carried him to the front of the house. Colt drawn, he inched to the open door, where he strained to hear any sound from within. There was nothing. The only thing filling his ears was the pounding of his own pulse.

Sucking in a breath, he poked his head around the doorframe and looked inside. The door opened onto a parlor. No one was there. He started into the house, then caught himself. He was up against Jacob Mason, the man in black, the invisible man who hid himself in the background. In spite of his desperate need to find Lisa, this was no time to throw caution to the wind. A dead Ranger would be of no use to the young woman.

Aiming the Colt's muzzle everywhere that his gaze alighted, the Ranger stepped inside the house. Nothing. No shadow moved within the shadows. No one crouched ready to spring from behind the furniture.

He crept toward the light that came from a door at the opposite end of the parlor. Again he cautiously peered beyond the doorway into a narrow hall that he remembered led to three bedrooms. The lamp's yellow glow came from Lisa's bedroom at the end of the hall. His Colt leveled against attack, Cody strode into the hallway. Still there was nothing—no sound, no movement.

Stifling the urge to run to Lisa's bedroom, the Ranger moved to the first bedroom and threw open the door. It appeared empty. His gaze probed the near blackness. He found nothing. Closing the door, Cody moved to the second bedroom. Once more there was nothing, no trace of Jacob Mason. That left Lisa's bedroom.

His grip tightening on the Colt, he headed toward the open door. Mason had to be inside waiting. Every instinct told Cody that the madman would be there with his victim. The Ranger remembered the loaded shotgun Lisa kept by her bed since the night they ran into the man in black. A blast of double-aught buckshot could cut a man in two at close quarters, if a man made himself an easy target.

Cody had no intention of doing that.

Pressing himself flat against a wall, he called, "Mason, it's over. Come on out with your hands high."

There was no answer.

"Mason, let Lisa go and come out," Cody yelled, trying again. "Give yourself up."

Mason remained silent.

Cody drew a mental picture of the bedroom beyond the open door. Lisa's bed was on the left side of the room. On the right stood a small dressing table and chair. Mason, shotgun in hand, could be on either side. It was a toss-up as to where he'd position himself. The only thing certain was that if he wasn't coming out, the Ranger had to go in. The longer Mason held Lisa captive, the less likely it was that she'd come out of this alive. If it wasn't already too late.

The left side, Cody decided. The bed offered more cover than a dressing table. Mason would be to the left. But what if he'd guessed wrong?

He didn't dwell on that possibility. Instead he leapt forward, throwing himself into the bedroom and hitting the hardwood floor in a roll that ended in a crouch. He swung around, right arm fully extended and Colt raised.

Nothing. There was no waiting shotgun blast, no Jacob Mason. Except for Lisa, who lay tied spread-eagle atop her bed, the room was empty. Cody pushed to his feet, confusion reeling in his brain.

Where the hell was Mason?

He stepped to the bed. Lisa's breast rose and fell in a gentle rhythm. An ugly bruise was forming under her chin where she'd apparently been struck and rendered unconscious. Cody allowed himself the luxury of a moment's relief. He hadn't come too late. Except for the bruised jaw and a few fine, crosshatched cuts beneath her collarbone that were no deeper than thorn scratches, she was unharmed— or at least so her body appeared. Cody quickly reminded himself that Mason still presented a great threat, one that precluded admiring Lisa's naked form.

He started to holster the Colt and free the bowie knife on his left hip when he stopped himself. Lisa's bonds could wait. For the moment she was safe, and he wanted to make certain she stayed that way. Until he had Mason, there'd be no guarantees of anyone's safety.

A breeze set the curtains fluttering on one of the bedroom's windows, catching Cody's attention. As he walked toward the open window he concluded that while he was entering the house, Mason had opened a window and slipped outside. He couldn't have gotten far.

Cody pushed aside the curtain and leaned out to peer toward the bunkhouse and barn. He hadn't heard a horse, which meant that Mason was on foot. He wouldn't get away this night. Tonight the man in black's reign of terror would end.

Suddenly two arms shot up from beneath the window. Viselike hands clamped on to his shoulders, the fingers digging in like claws. The hands yanked the Ranger from his feet, pulling him out the window. His right wrist slammed against the windowsill as he was hauled through and sent hurtling to the ground. His fingers went numb, and the Colt fell from his hand.

Whether the pistol had dropped on the bedroom floor or on the ground beneath the window, Cody didn't know, though there wasn't much time to think about retrieving the weapon. The Ranger hit the ground facedown, and the impact drove the air from his lungs and dizziness into his head.

He forced himself to move. Reaching down with his tingling right hand, he found the hilt of the bowie knife. As he rolled to his back, he wrenched the long-bladed knife free of its scabbard.

It was too late. Mason bounded toward him, leaping like a mountain panther. His right foot lashed out, driving into the Ranger's wrist. The bowie knife sailed from Cody's numb hand, lost in the night.

Mason's arms snaked out again, once more clamping to the Ranger's shoulders. His madness had imbued his wiry body with seemingly superhuman strength, and though inches shorter and many pounds lighter than the man he attacked, Mason held Cody fast.

With no feeling in his right hand, Cody balled his left and drove it into Mason's face with all the strength he could muster. On more than one occasion such a blow had laid out a barroom brawler. Mason merely shook off the punch and grinned. Cody struck again, but Mason remained unshaken. He chuckled and heaved the Ranger aside like a rag doll.

Cody slammed into the ground onto his left shoulder. He groaned as pain lanced through his arm. Ignoring the pain as best he could, he twisted to his back.

"Do you understand?" Mason asked. "Can you see how you have been delivered into my hands?" The preacher came at Cody in slow, steady steps. "You were to have been just a minor puppet in my wonderful play. Now you will be so much more. Now you will be a featured player.

Now you will fill a role granted only a chosen few. What an honor for you, Ranger!"

Mason's words were the babbling of the insane. But a madman posed more danger than a sane man. Gritting his teeth to fight past the pain in his arm, Cody struggled to his feet. Forcing the numb fingers of his right hand apart, he interlocked them with those of his left. Swinging his arms back over his shoulders, he sprang at Mason, swinging his hands like a hammer and throwing the weight of his body behind the blow. Solidly, he slammed into Mason's temple.

The man staggered slightly but kept coming, answering the attack with a right fist driven into Cody's belly. Air rushed from the Ranger's lungs; his body doubled over. Mason's left fist hammered into Cody's jaw, snapping his head back. Then there was the punishing right fist again; this time it pounded the side of his face. And the left fist drove to his opposite cheek.

Cody backstepped to escape the relentless assault. But there was no escape. Mason's fists kept hammering, finding their way through his flailing arms. Blood filled the Ranger's mouth, and more blood trickled from his nostrils. He felt as helpless as a child before the strength of this lunatic.

Cody had countless times accepted the possibility of a bullet ending his life. Never had he considered being pounded to death. He suddenly thought of Lisa still tied to her bed. He should have cut the ropes binding her.

Then a dark wave rose, sucking him down into it.

Cody awakened to pain searing his chest—pain far sharper than the throbbing of his face, head, and arms. The pain yanked him from the black pit of unconsciousness into soft yellow light. Groaning, he forced his swollen eyes to open. His bound hands were wrenched over his head, and he was strung from a ceiling beam like a side of meat. His shirt had been cut apart, exposing his chest.

"You're awake. That's good."

Mason was standing inches away from him. In his right

hand he held a curved-bladed skinning knife. A line of crimson defined the sharp edge. He suddenly reached out with the knife and drew it across the Ranger's chest.

Cody gasped, unable to escape the hot agony that seared his flesh.

"First you will satisfy my hunger, then the girl." Mason stared at the skinning knife, watching a drop of blood roll down the steel.

Breathing hard, Cody looked up at the rope. Mason had done an expert job. The Ranger couldn't see any way of getting free. Another stab of pain jerked Cody's head back as Mason drew the knife across his chest again. He struggled fiercely, but he couldn't escape the blade. He merely dangled like a marionette.

The knife flashed once more, this time slicing deeper.

"You goddamn bastard!" Cody roared, partly to disguise the cry of pain when the blade raked over a rib.

Mason chuckled. "Your words cannot touch me, Ranger. Nothing can touch me. Or hadn't you noticed?"

A soft groan came from behind Cody. Mason looked back at the open doorway, and a grotesque grin spread across his face. "Lisa is waking. Good. She will hear you as you leave this life, and she can prepare herself for what is to come." His grin widened. "May I share with you my plans for Lisa after you're no longer of any use to me? I think you'll enjoy them. I know I will."

Enraged, Cody tried kicking out, but Mason sidestepped easily. Then his wrist flicked, and the blade sliced into Cody's chest. The Ranger tried wrenching to one side. The action was futile. Again the knife lashed out.

Suddenly Mason straightened, and he cocked his head. "What's this? Do I hear another joining us?"

Cody heard it now, approaching hooves. Had Captain Vickery or Sheriff Whittington ridden after him? Surely they would have!

Mason turned and stared out the open door of the ranch house. "Yes, yes, it's your Captain Vickery. How considerate of him to join us. There will be three giving me pleasure this night."

Cody had to act before Mason lured Vickery into his web

of insanity. While Mason's back was turned as he watched out the front door, the Ranger's fingers strained upward, wrapping themselves around the rope. Summoning every ounce of strength remaining in his weakening body, he arched back and swung his legs up as high as he could and locked them around Mason's neck.

"No!" Mason screeched. "No!"

Cody squeezed as hard as he could. He had no hope of strangling the man, but he might hold him until Vickery came to his aid.

Mason's right arm shot upward, burying the skinning knife in Cody's right thigh. The driving pain brought a howl from the Ranger's throat, but his legs remained locked desperately around Mason's neck. He groaned as Mason wrenched the blade free and drove it into his leg again.

Cody twisted violently to escape the fiery agony, and Mason, his boots slipping on the polished surface of the hardwood floor, fell sharply. A sickening crack filled the room, and the preacher's body abruptly went limp.

Cody was uncertain of time's passage, but to his dazed and pain-riddled brain it seemed like hours before he realized what had happened. Mason's neck had snapped.

Unlocking his ankles, Cody let Mason's lifeless body spill to the floor. It was over. The madman was dead.

"Cody! Cody, you in there?" Vickery's gravelly voice called out.

Cody lifted his head and opened his mouth. But his answer was drowned in another wave that pulled him back down into blackness.

CHAPTER

‖‖‖‖‖‖‖‖‖‖‖‖‖‖‖‖‖‖‖‖ **15** ‖‖‖‖‖‖‖‖‖‖‖‖‖‖‖‖‖‖‖‖

Doc Clancy, San Angelo's physician, carefully reband-aged Cody's chest and then stood to stare down at his patient, stretched out on the bed.

"It looks good," he announced, pleased with his handi-work. "There's no sign of infection, and the stitches are holding. You lost a lot of blood, so you'll be weak for a while, but I'd say in two weeks you should be in good shape. That is, if you rest for those two weeks. You've got some deep cuts. You don't want to go opening them. Take everything slow and easy."

"I'll see that he does," Lisa Kingston said as she entered the bedroom carrying a tray laden with a pot of coffee, cups, and a plate of freshly fried doughnuts.

"Doughnuts! I do love doughnuts!" Captain Vickery said as he pushed from the chair beside Cody's bed and snatched a sugary morsel from the tray before Lisa could place it on the nightstand.

Lisa smiled at the captain, then asked the doctor, "Would you care for a cup of coffee?"

Clancy shook his head. "Nelly Watson is expecting. I'd best be on my way back to town. Thank you anyway, though, Lisa." He removed his hat from a bedpost, then faced Cody once more. "Remember what I said. Get plenty of rest, and take it slow and easy."

"I promise," Cody replied.

Clancy smiled and left the room.

"You ought to try one of these, Cody. They're excellent,"

Vickery said as he stuffed the last bite of the doughnut into his mouth and took another from the plate. "Reminds me of doughnuts I once had in San Antonio when I was a mite younger. . . ."

Lisa held out the plate, and Cody accepted one of the confections. He bit into it and pronounced it the best he'd ever eaten.

Lisa laughed as she poured them all coffee. "I have a feeling that just about anything will taste like the best you've ever eaten. I think you're just glad to still be alive."

Cody smiled. "I can't argue with that. I thought for sure I was a dead man two nights ago."

Vickery's good-natured expression abruptly vanished. "I wonder what made him do it. What brought on the insanity that made him butcher so many people?"

Cody slowly shook his head. "I've tried to make sense out of all he said, but there was no sense to be made. I reckon we'll never know."

Lisa shivered. "I don't believe I want to know."

"Well, the only thing we know for sure," Vickery put in, "is that we got the right man this time. Thank God we found out before another man fell victim to Mason's madness."

"Yes, how is Lieutenant Harper?" Cody asked.

"He's all right. He's back at Fort Concho. The Army offered to reassign him, but he's stayin' in San Angelo. I think he feels like he needs to prove himself to the town. He's a strong 'un. He'll do it."

"And you, Captain? What are your plans?" Lisa asked.

"I've got supplies loaded in my saddlebags right outside. Now that I know Cody'll be all right, I reckon it's time for me to head back to Del Rio."

Lisa stood. "How about a few doughnuts to keep you company?"

Vickery chuckled. "I'd like that." The Ranger captain rose as Lisa left the room, then looked down at Cody. "Doc said you'd be yourself in two weeks, so in three I expect you back at headquarters." He glanced back at the doorway, then leaned close and whispered in Cody's ear, "Meanwhile, you watch yourself. That little filly can be mighty determined. If you don't look out, she just might try to rope and brand you. I'd hate to lose a good man."

Cody grinned. "I'll be careful. And Cap'n, you watch out for yourself. You have to pass through Eldorado on the way back. There's a widow there who might try to dry-gulch you."

"Don't you worry about me none, son." A distant look came over Vickery's face, and he smiled slyly. "However, it mightn't be a bad idea to stop by and pay my respects while I'm in town." In the wink of an eye Vickery's usual stern expression returned, and he headed from the room. Pausing in the doorway, he said, "Three weeks, Cody, I want you back in Del Rio in three weeks."

"I'll be there."

Cody leaned back into the softness of the pillows under his head. He shivered at the sight of the ceiling beams. A Ranger always trod close to death, but this time he felt as though he'd taken a step across the line. Had the captain and Lisa not been there to pull him back, he'd be lying six feet under right now. It wasn't a pleasant thing to have one's mortality thrown in one's face. Particularly by a madman.

Lisa returned to the room and said, "Well, your captain's off. How's my patient?"

"Alive," Cody replied. "And that's a hell of a good thing to be."

An impish light sparkled in Lisa's eyes as she crossed to the bed and stared down at Cody. "Two weeks, Doc Clancy said. Have you got any idea what we can do for those two weeks?"

Cody grinned, knowing full well what was running through the auburn-haired beauty's mind. "Whatever it is, it'll have to be like the Doc said: slow and easy. I feel like I'm wrapped in barbed wire."

"Slow and easy." Lisa nodded as her hands tucked behind her back to free the hooks of her dress. "I think I can handle that."

CODY'S LAW: BOOK 11

RED MOON'S RAID

by Matthew S. Hart

Returning from patrol, Texas Ranger Sam Cody is pinned down behind rocks by Comanche renegades led by Twisted Hawk, an infamous war chief. After what seems like an eternity, night falls, and Cody makes a getaway—briefly. The pursuing Indians catch up with him, and he's certain his time has come. But a group of cowhands ride in and send the Indians fleeing.

Back in Del Rio, the rest of Ranger Company C is battling an attack by a band of outlaws. The ruthless owlhoots gun down anyone in their path as they loot the town, and as they ride off they grab five women, including Lieutenant Whitcomb's daughter. With the bloodcurdling yip of a Comanche the leader shouts, "Del Rio will never forget the visit of Red Moon!"

The lawmen track the raiders, but the trail is lost when a sandstorm blows up, and Captain Vickery orders their return to town. Whitcomb is left with nothing to go on and all of West Texas to search, but he vows to stay out until he finds his daughter, even if he has to do it alone. Cody volunteers to join him in the search.

By a stroke of luck they locate the outlaws—but their luck sours when an overeager Army shavetail, also in pursuit of Red Moon's gang, ruins Cody's plan of attack. The three men are imprisoned with the captive women—and Cody wonders grimly if any of them will get out of this alive.

**Read RED MOON'S RAID, on sale
wherever Bantam Books are sold.**

CODY'S LAW

Matthew S. Hart

He rides alone for a breed that stands apart. He wears the badge of the Texas Rangers and a pair of silver spurs. He is the master of every weapon of the West—white man's or Indian's—and the servant of a fiercely held code of right and wrong. His name is Cody. The Rangers made Texas a land of law. Men like Cody made the Rangers a legend.

❑ *California Glory* (28970-5 $4.99/$5.99 in Canada) Riots and strikes rock America's cities as workers demand freedom, fairness, and justice for all.

❑ *Hawaii Heritage* (29414-8 $5.50/$6.50 in Canada) Seeds of revolution turn the island paradise into a land of brutal turmoil and seething unrest.

❑ *Sierra Triumph* (29750-3 $5.50/$6.50 in Canada) A battle that goes beyond that of the sexes challenges the ideals of a nation and one remarkable family.

❑ *Yukon Justice* (29763-5 $5.50/$6.50 in Canada) As gold fever sweeps the nation, a great migration to the Yukon Territory of Canada begins.

❑ *Pacific Destiny* (56149-9 $5.99/$6.99 in Canada) From the tropics of Cuba to the Philippines, the Holt family is on the threshold of the American Century.

And now
WAGONS WEST:
THE FRONTIER TRILOGY
From Dana Fuller Ross

❑ *Westward!* (29402-4 $5.50/$6.50 in Canada) The clock is turned back with this early story of the Holts, men and women who lived through the most rugged era of American exploration.

❑ *Expedition!* (29403-2 $5.50/$6.50 in Canada) In the heart of a majestic land, Clay Holt leads a perilous expedition up the Yellowstone River.

❑ *Outpost!* (29400-8 $5.50/$6.50 in Canada) Clay heads to Canada to bring a longtime enemy to justice.

Available at your local bookstore or use this page to order.

Send to: Bantam Books, Dept. LE 13
         2451 S. Wolf Road
         Des Plaines, IL 60018

Please send me the items I have checked above. I am enclosing $_____ (please add $2.50 to cover postage and handling). Send check or money order, no cash or C.O.D.'s, please.

Mr./Ms._____

Address_____

City/State_____Zip_____

Please allow four to six weeks for delivery.

Prices and availability subject to change without notice.   LE 13B 1/94